PROVEN

ACES HIGH MC - CEDAR FALLS
BOOK 3

CHRISTINE MICHELLE

Cover Design ©2025 Christine Michelle
ISBN: 979-8-89706-018-4

ABOUT THE BOOK

I followed my heart from San Diego, California to Cedar Falls, West Virginia.
Too bad the woman I followed wasn't worth the trip.
Thankfully, I had my job, new friends - which consisted of an entire motorcycle club I'd fallen into - and my newfound responsibility for a family that was torn apart by needless tragedy.
I might not have followed the right woman to Cedar Falls, but it led me to a single mother and her son, both of whom managed to capture my heart.
Between her ex and mine, we had a lot of baggage to wade through. That extra weight around our necks almost cost us each other and something far more important - her son.
There was no doubt that I was brought to Cedar Falls, West Virginia for a reason. I was meant to save the boy, find the woman, and become a part of a new family that my had my back through it all.

- Friends to Lovers
- Found Family
- Single Mom
- MC Romance
- Romantic Suspense
- Firefighter/Paramedic

TRIGGER WARNINGS

- Strong language
- Violence
- Car Accident
- Deaths of children (secondary characters)
- Kidnapping
- Murder
- Cheating (not by main character)
- Sexual Situations described on page
- Potential other triggers not listed here.

AHMC
CEDAR FALLS
3

Surfer & Gillian

PROLOGUE

Something was off in a major way as I sat my bag down on the chair next to the front door and glanced around for my girlfriend, Kayla.

There were things missing from the room. I couldn't put my finger exactly what was gone, but I knew there were void spaces where shit used to be. A picture of us from our first date used to sit on the entertainment center. It was gone along with all the movies, music, and video games that had once been visible in the open cabinets underneath.

"What in the hell?" I muttered the question to myself since Kayla was missing in action somewhere in the apartment we'd shared for the past eleven months. Just as I was about to explore, I saw her head poke out from around the bedroom doorjamb.

"Oh, good, you're home!" she squealed. A hard knot clenched tightly in my gut. With Kayla that squeal could mean she was horny and about to jump my bones – which I wouldn't be opposed to – or it could mean that she'd done something stupid. I sighed as I wondered if she opened another credit account in both of our names without my permission.

It was something she seemed more inclined to do the longer we were together. Her penchant for doing just that had warranted me putting a freeze on my credit account to keep it from happening again. If only I hadn't lifted the freeze briefly to get the loan for my bike.

"Kayla, there are things miss-" I didn't even get the full statement out before her body slammed into mine. It was obvious she expected me to read her fucking mind and catch her as she flung herself in my direction. Sadly for her, she forgot that I was coming off a forty-eight-hour shift with Emergency Medical Services.

Instead of me catching her, and those long legs of hers wrapping around my waist as she'd obviously intended, she nearly knocked me off my feet as our bodies collided and hers slipped to the ground in a thud. The pout of her lips and furrow in her brow tipped me off to the fact that she wasn't happy about it.

I wasn't a fucking mind reader, though.

Before Kayla could say a word, I picked her up and then slid her a full arm's length back from where I stood. My girl-friend wasn't fooling anyone. Her little full-body attack was meant to distract me, even if it didn't go quite the way she had planned.

"Just got off shift, Kay, my reaction time isn't all there. It was a fuckin' long shift."

Her pout didn't dissipate. As usual with Kayla, other people's lack of energy didn't factor into her plans. She had grown up a spoiled rotten princess in a huge house near Old Town in San Diego. Her parents had reason to cut her off financially just before she graduated college, though she'd never bothered filling me in on why they had done so.

Not that she shouldn't be fiscally responsible for herself now that she was an adult, but she still tried to live at their financial level, and that wasn't easily done on my EMT's salary plus the pay she earned as a phlebotomist.

I still almost chuckled every time I thought about her job. The princess sticking people with needles and pulling their blood from their body had to be a sight. I had yet to see her in action, though. I felt bad for her patients without ever having seen her skill, or lack thereof, because she could be a frosty bitch when doing something she disliked. And one thing was for sure, Kayla didn't appreciate having to work for her money.

"I have good news to share," her pouty tone told me I should probably sit down before she got started. There was no telling what Kay thought of as good news.

"Well?" I questioned as I scooted my bag off the chair then plopped into it as the bag came to rest at my feet.

Kayla perked up as if my monotone, one-word question was the segue she needed to get into heaven, not to start a conversation. I had a feeling this wasn't going to be something she should smack me with the moment I walked through the door after a very full forty-eight hours shift.

"My grandma died, and she left me a house and a bunch of money!" she shrieked excitedly. I frowned at the outburst, considering she mentioned the death of a family member in there somewhere.

"Kay, I'm sorry to hear about your grandma," I started, but she waved off my concern with the swipe of her hand in the air like it meant nothing.

"That's not the important thing, Gray. Did you hear the part about where I inherited a house and tons of money?" she asked. It was as if she thought I was daft for putting the death of a family member ahead of some inherited fortune.

I sighed and scrubbed my hand down my face. "Okay, that's, well... that's news. I guess our lease is up in another month, so that's good timing if you wanted to move into your grandma's house," I started wearily.

"I knew it!" she shrieked again, causing my head to throb as she bounced around the living room like a little bunny on crack. "I knew you'd be okay with moving, and all the crap that will go with it."

Uh-oh. Alarm bells started ringing then. "Where is this house, Kay?"

"Um," she hesitated, biting her bottom lip for effect. It was a gesture I'd found sexy when we first started dating. Over time, I noticed how she used it as a tool to manipulate, and not because it was a natural thing for her to do. I sighed again. Whatever she was bound to say next probably was not going to make me happy.

"Well, see, the thing is there's a teeny, tiny stipulation in her will that states I have to live in the house for one year in order to collect the money." She started to pace, and before I could ask what was wrong with the house that it would cause this reaction she continued. "And um, I already found a job there, and have everything set. I even started packing."

"Kayla, you already found a job where? Where is this house?"

"Cedar Falls, West Virginia." It was said as a statement that brokered no argument.

"West fucking where, again?" I asked, completely flummoxed that she was laying this on me like she'd had all the time in the world to prep and I should already be up to speed and onboard with what was going down.

"There's no need to curse at me, Gray!" She threw her hands up, her strawberry blond locks with their chunky curls bounced around her shoulders as she did so. This movement also caused her braless tits to jiggle just so. An outsider would think this was all cute, sexy, and done without thought. That outsider looking in would be wrong. These were more of Kay's go-to moves to distract from whatever shit was flying out of her mouth.

"The house is in Cedar Falls, West Virginia. I don't know why the old bat moved there to begin with, but she did, and the only way to get the house is to move and stay for a year. Then I can sell the house and collect the money, too. It's perfect. We can come back here or go wherever we want. I was thinking maybe Los Angeles or something more glamorous than San Diego when we come back." All of this was said without her taking a breath.

I stared at her and waited for to realize the thing she left out of her calculations. "What about my job?"

Again, she waved me off with a flip of her neatly manicured fingers. I noted that they looked professionally done again, even after we discussed the fact that we couldn't really afford frivolous expenses after her last run through of the credit cards she maxed out.

Some of the cards she got were in my name even though I never applied for them, hence the credit freeze I'd had to obtain. I blew out a frustrated breath. I couldn't afford to renew the lease on this apartment without someone to split the bills with me. Kayla had driven off most of my friends with her antics. My partner at work was a female with a husband and three kids. The rest of the guys had cramped quarters for living arrangements, but ones they were all happy with. Damn it. She had just put me in one hell of a bind.

"Kayla, if I go with you, I need to give my work notice. I also need to have employment set up ahead of time, so I don't have too big a lapse in paychecks, especially since I'm paying on my bike and paying off the damage you did to cards I never fuckin' ordered."

It was her turn to blow out a frustrated breath now. "Jesus, Gray, you act like I'm putting you out. This is a huge opportunity that I simply can't turn down. Once the year is up, I will be rolling in dough!" She was squealing excitedly again, forgetting the serious shit I was just bringing up.

"Kayla, come back down to earth with the rest of us mortals, and listen. I need to know when we're supposed to be moving. We have less than forty-five days to re-up the lease here or get the hell out. You're already packing shit, some of which belongs to me. I need to know what exactly is going on. Sit down, stop the drama, and be real for five fuckin' minutes."

Talking to Kay about anything of substance was like

talking to a five-year-old most days. Only, I would expect that five-year-old children behaved better.

Kayla poked her bottom lip out again, which really did nothing but highlight her almost complete lack of an upper lip. Normally, she had it lined so heavily that you couldn't tell as much. Packing must have distracted her from putting a full face of makeup on. She was also pulling it tight while jutting out the bottom, so it disappeared completely. Damn it. Her distraction techniques were working, just not in the way she hoped they did.

"Okay, I have to be there in ten days. I'm packing everything and taking it with me. If you need a couple extra days for work, then so be it. I have to be there on the twelfth or else I lose everything."

"How long have you known about this?"

She looked away guiltily for a moment before her eyes met mine again with a hint of defiance. As she answered, I was sure she hadn't meant to let me see that. "Two months," she stated sweetly as she adjusted her face that her smile matched the "you can't be mad at me" tone.

"Two months?" I questioned on a growl. "You've known about this for two months, are scheduled to be there in ten days, and you are just now telling me about it?"

She shrugged her bony shoulders. "I um, wasn't sure you would want to come with me. I wanted to make sure I had everything set ahead of time just in case."

"You wanted to make sure you had everything set, *FOR YOU*!" I reiterated, emphasizing the last two words. "What about me? What if I wanted to go with you? You've left me no time. What if I don't want to go? You've already started packing *my* shit. Is it packed separately or thrown in willy-nilly with your own stuff?"

"You don't want to go?" she questioned looking truly taken aback.

"I didn't say that, Kay!" I almost yelled since completely losing my shit at this point didn't seem that far off. "I'm saying you dropped this on me at the last fucking minute when you've known for two goddamn months!"

"I was just trying to plan everything so you wouldn't have much, besides your job, to worry about." She got up and came to sit her ass down on my lap as she brushed the tip of her breast across my cheek.

"Baby," she whined. "I want us to do this together. I'll be able to pay off all those credit cards, and even your bike as a thank you and an apology for the whole credit card thing."

That part of her plan had some merit. I would love to have my bike paid for free and clear. Something I would have been able to do if I hadn't had to tap into my savings to bail her ass out of the credit card fiasco that she caused last time.

"Ten days, huh?" She nodded her head vigorously and started a little mini bounce session in my lap. "Fuck, dude!" I hissed as her bony ass came down in just the wrong spot.

"You know I hate when you call me 'dude' or 'bro,' Gray."

"Really, Kay?" I huffed and gave her a stern look.

She tossed her hands up in the air as if she was giving up, or giving in, two things she never did. "Does this mean you're coming?"

"It's not looking like I have much choice in the matter. You'll be there." Yes, she was annoying me more lately, but I still loved her. She put up with my shit when I came home with fresh nightmares from my time in the Army. I'd wake up screaming, and she'd rub my head and coo sweet things to me until I drifted back off to sleep. It almost felt like I owed her my loyalty for seeing me through that fucked up transition period.

There were things about her that redeemed the spoiled bitch routine she liked to hide behind. There were glimpses of the woman I hoped she'd move further toward, but only time would tell. For now, it looked like I was moving to West-By-God-Virginia, and I had to get a handle on that situation quickly.

1. DISILLUSIONED

TEN DAYS LATER, I WAS STARING UP AT THE OLD WHITE FARMHOUSE with aging gray shutters. It appeared as though they may have been blue at some point. The house needed a lot of work. It seemed that Kayla's grandmother hadn't enlisted anyone to help her with upkeep in her final years. I groaned aloud as we stared at the money pit in front of us.

Kayla's nose crinkled up in disgust, too. "What the hell?" she shouted at me as if I could magically produce the answers to her questions.

"It did not look like this in the pictures I saw. What's up with this grass? Why hasn't it been mowed at all? My God, it's like three feet tall in spots where there's actually grass or weeds or whatever that stuff is." She complained as if she'd be the one to tackle the jungle of a lawn we were faced with.

"Well, I'm guessing once your grandma died two months ago you never bothered to hire anyone to care for the lawn until you could get here to do it."

Again, her nose crinkled as her head slid back in a

shocked movement. "Why on earth would I be responsible for hiring someone to care for the lawn? There are people for that."

"Kayla, when you're a homeowner, you are '*the people*' meant to take care of that shit," I groaned in frustration. "If you had told me about all this to begin with, I would have pointed out all those finer details you seem to be clueless about."

"Not this again!" she huffed as she pulled her small overnight bag out of the truck, leaving everything else behind. "You need to get over the short notice bullshit and start helping out around here. Obviously, this place is going to need a lot of work, and I need to take care of too many other things."

I stared at her back as she moved to the front porch and gingerly stepped up, thinking maybe the weathered boards wouldn't hold her. It was obvious they were solid, and only in need of new stain and sealer. I ignored her and took inventory of all the things we were going to need.

The detached one-car garage would suffice for my bike, for now, but not for long since I didn't want the thing collapsing on my baby. It was not large enough to hold my truck, and Kayla had never owned a car since she lost her license in college – yet another thing she failed to mention until she told me I'd need to get her back and forth to work.

She told me this on the trip out here when I asked her to take over driving for a while, because I was dog-ass tired and hoping to save on another hotel stay. Unlike my clueless girlfriend, I figured we'd have a few extra expenses when we got to Cedar Falls that we hadn't factored in. Expenses like the lawn mower we now needed to buy. Hell, at this point I was tempted to hire someone to take care of the first round of jungle taming, because this was going to take for-fucking-ever with just me doing the work.

Kayla had disappeared inside the house and swiftly pranced right back out, hands on her hips and scowl firmly set in her normally pretty face.

"Are you going to stand there all day, or are you going to start to bring things in?"

I noted that she didn't come out to help unload the truck. Nope. Princess Kayla turned her ass back around and marched right back into the house. The screen door banged shut behind her which caused it to come off the top hinge and hang awkwardly as it clapped back and forth with the momentum.

"Oh my God! You need to fix that!" Kayla shouted.

"Why did I come here?" I asked the air around me, as if something in nature would find a way to send an answer. It didn't. I turned back to the truck, grabbed my bag, the box in the back labeled "bathroom supplies," and then toted them into the house. I set the box and my bag on the couch to the right of the door after I made my way inside.

It was a good thing I didn't attempt to bring a bigger load, because Kayla hadn't been waiting to open the door for me. I sighed as I looked around. At least it seemed cozy and well-tended on the inside, minus all the dust that had collected.

"Ew, all her old lady stuff is still sitting around every-where," Kayla called out from somewhere deeper in the house. "There's nasty spoiled food in the fridge," she was saying when she came back into view. "You're going to have to take care of that."

"And what are you taking care of, Kayla? So far, you've ordered me to tame the jungle without a fuckin' weed eater, let alone a lawn mower or a bush hog or whatever it's gonna take for that job. Then I need to fix the door you just broke, because you couldn't be bothered to shut it gently, and I have to unpack the truck before I take care of either of those things. Then you want me to deal with cleaning the fridge, too? What the fuck are you doing while I get everything done by myself?"

She flinched back at my tone. "I'm, um, looking around to see if anything she had in this house is salvageable," Kayla answered as if taking inventory of the shit her grandmother left behind was priority.

"No!" My tone brooked no argument. "First, you're going to get your ass out to the truck and help unload it, because you don't have servants here and I'm not a fuckin' slave. Then, you're going to take care of disposing of the rotten food in the fridge while I deal with the door and the lawn. After that, we're going through the house together and making a priority list of shit that's going to need tending to, so we know what we're throwing money at first."

"Throwing money at?"

"You see this house? You don't get shit taken care of soon it's going to fall to pieces around you."

She glanced around, wrinkled nose and furrowed brow dominating her features again. "We only have to stay here and make it work for a year. I'm not throwing a bunch of unnecessary money at this place. It's nasty. I don't plan on staying a minute longer than necessary."

"Do you plan on getting any money for it when you try to sell in a year?"

"Of course. The internet said the house is valued at $260,000."

"Was," I said as I made another cursory glance around the place.

"What?"

"It was valued at $260,000, probably in its prime before it fell into disrepair. You'd be lucky to sell this place for $70,000 right now. Her surprised, horrified gasp made me chuckle.

"B-but, the lawyer said-"

I cut her off. "The lawyer was reading off a sheet of paper with information probably plugged in from the same Internet browser search you did. He wasn't looking at this place in person. Something else that should have been done in the two months you didn't tell me about this shit going down. We could have made a trip out here to scope it out and see if it was worth the hassle. You still haven't told me how much money you're supposed to get once the year is up."

"Maybe because I want to know you're with me because you love me, and not because of my money," she commented back snidely.

"You don't have any money, Kay, and I'm already with you." Sometimes I wondered what I ever saw in her. Honestly, there were more times I felt that way now than times I didn't. I still wasn't sure what possessed me to follow her here, except that there was this feeling in my gut that I needed to. Today, I was wondering what was wrong with my gut instincts. "You don't even have any savings set aside to do any of the repairs or buy any of the things we're going to need here."

"That's because when you paid the credit cards off you only paid the ones off that were in your name too," she scoffed.

"Yeah, because I never fuckin' ordered them and didn't want that hit on my credit. It also blew through my savings to do it." I didn't bother to tell her that I had most of my savings locked up in investments that were quite lucrative. I knew if I ever did, she'd blow through that too, and I was banking on that money for sending my kids to college one day, and for retirement and whatnot. Those things Kayla definitely wasn't ready to even think about, and honestly, I was beginning to wonder if she ever would be ready.

It was then that Kayla collapsed into the dusty chair, forcing a plume of filth up to billow up around her which in turn caused her to sneeze. After the sneeze her tears started. They were not her usual drama tears she used to get her way. They were real. "This isn't what my life was supposed to look like," she lamented between sobs. "Why did my dad do this to me?"

"Hate to tell you sweetheart, but most kids don't start out with a trust fund in hand. Just about everyone I've ever known has had to work for whatever they have, not have it handed to them."

"I work!" She shouted.

"Yes, you do, and there's nothing wrong with your job, how much you make, or the rest of your life. The only thing wrong is in YOUR head where you think you should be living so far beyond your means that you can't appreciate the things you have that you worked for. It's never enough for you."

"I grew up having everything!" She shouted at me, face turning red with her anger. "I had every damn thing I could want with the snap of a finger. It's not fair that it was all taken from me. Just because there was a scandal with me and my married professor," she ranted in between her sobs. I stilled. This was the first I was hearing about why she had been cut off. "I got rid of the kid, and daddy cleaned up the mess I made. He didn't need to turn me out too. Who cares if he went to school with the professor's wife? He basically acted like that woman meant more than I did. I was a victim too!"

"You were involved with your married professor? Did you know he was married?"

"Of course, I did! I just told you she was a friend of my dad," she snapped.

"Jesus, Kayla!" I spat out disgusted with her. "If you can't figure out where you went wrong with that situation there's no helping you." I wasn't touching on the fact that she'd mentioned a kid with complete disregard, and I had a feeling she was talking about her own baby. I may have made a mistake coming here, but I'd already shipped my things, found a job, and I was going to have to stick this out for a little bit until I could find a place of my own. I also had some morals and didn't plan to leave Kayla high and dry after agreeing to come with her. Whether she deserved my loyalty or not, didn't matter. It was about making sure I did the right thing.

Changing the subject, I started forming a plan. "Let's forget about all that and start thinking about how we're going to get you a driver's license, a car, and how we're going to fix the main things in the house that need tended to so it's livable."

Kayla glanced up at me between wet lashes and gave me a small smile. "You don't hate me too?"

"I don't hate you, Kay," I informed her. Though, if I were going to be completely honest, she had finally killed any of the old feelings I had for her. Now, I only felt obligation. I'd get her set, so she could function on her own, and then I would be out of this mess for good.

2. DEATH, BEER, AND A PROPOSITION

THREE WEEKS HAD GONE BY SINCE I MOVED TO CEDAR FALLS WITH Kayla. Three weeks and she had made zero progress in getting her shit together. Three weeks, and I was about to lose my damn mind with her bullshit, frivolous spending when we had so much to do to get her house straightened out, especially since it quickly became obvious that a hot water heater was needed since the other one wasn't working at all.

Thankfully, I was able to shower at the station. Kayla bitched about that too, but I made her save for the water heater on her own since I had purchased the lawn mower, weed eater, taken care of the insanely overgrown yard, fixed the screen door, and ended up buying a new refrigerator too.

The bright spot in my life was the fact that I loved my job with Cedar Falls Fire and Rescue. The guys I worked with were amazing, including one everyone referred to as Smoke. We didn't interact that much since he was on the fire side and I was rescue, but I had admired his bike a few times when I pulled in next to it. He had a sparkling beauty of a Harley Dyna Wide Glide. I'd never seen the wide glides up close and personal before. It was a beast of a bike, and according to the guys, and the patched vest Smoke put on at the end of every shift before he rolled out, he belonged to a local motorcycle club.

I had a buddy from the Army who went home to his MC family on the Oregon coast, different outfit, but same basic rules far as I could tell. He had attempted to get me to come with, saying they liked welcoming in vets, but I had met Kayla at that point, and had been infatuated at the time since she seemed to help calm the beastly nightmares that plagued me.

I had asked around if any of the guys at the station were looking for roommates or whatever, but so far there weren't any bites coming in, so it made me less inclined to get free of Kayla's shit. Not that I still wasn't thinking of getting clear of her, because I was. I just wasn't in a huge rush to do it just yet.

That was where my thoughts were stuck when the alarms started going off and our unit was dispatched. I had yet another failed nap down at the station thanks to my roaming thoughts and now some sort of traffic muck-up. Our engine was dispatched with us, which put a little more hustle in my step. If it was something simple, we would have gone in alone. I had this weird response to things throughout my whole life. Just before something major happened my gut would flip-flop in ways that made me feel all at once like I was going to be sick, and like there was a brick lodged in my stomach. The moment the alarms sounded, I felt it.

There was a tingle; an inkling of something more, and then there was just the empty pit of anticipation settled deep in my gut waiting to be filled. I had to put the strange feeling out of mind as I gathered up the bags in the back when Steph, my paramedic partner, got us close to the scene. Steph may have been the paramedic on board, but only because I hadn't been officially certified yet. I had more experience with actual emergency procedures in the field than she did, so she treated me as an equal even when she didn't have to. It also hadn't taken long for her to assess my skill level and realize she could trust me to do what needed doing without fucking it up.

The minute I jumped off the bus – our term for the ambulance – a man who stunk to high heaven of bourbon yanked at my arm. "Shaank crist yoww hew. Arms cut." He pointed down to where his arm was dripping blood as he slurred his words beyond recognition.

"Were you involved in the accident?" I asked.

He attempted to nod his head in confirmation, but overdid it, and ended up tipping forward, nearly taking us both down to the concrete as I took his weight. He didn't even try to right himself outside of flailing arms that clocked me in the eye one good time before I finally got him straight-ened back up. I pointed to the heap of a truck that had careened into the other vehicle. "Were you driving that one?"

He eyed me suspiciously. "Why yuz wannsta know?"

"I need to know what kind of glass cut you, so we know how to treat your arm," I lied. He again tried to bob his head, but I held him steady. "That one yours?" I asked again.

"Yup," he said while popping the p along with a bubble of spit. "Peez-s-shit's mine."

I flagged down a cop and passed the drunk off to him. "This guy said he was driving that truck," I pointed. "He smells like a distillery."

"Son of a bitch!" The cop hissed. I didn't stick around to see what happened after that. I had a job to do, and it sure as fuck wasn't to put the drunk who caused the accident first on my triage list. From the looks of the car they were attempting to peel apart I was needed elsewhere. When I got to the other vehicle my partner Stephanie had a female toddler out on the ground, and she was working on her.

"What's up, Steph?" I called as I moved in closer.

"I got the girl. The mom is still with us, though passed out. They're trying to cut her free, but you might want to crawl in the back and be ready to stabilize her. Do it from the passenger side. Three DOAs in the car, and it ain't pretty." The last couple words were muttered. Considering the fact that she was working on a child I had a sneaking suspicion of what I'd find inside the vehicle.

I had been right, unfortunately. There were two adults up front. The male driver was one of the DOAs. The female passenger was who Steph had referred to as mom since she was a female, possibly late twenties or early thirties. Behind the driver was what appeared to be a kindergarten-aged male child. He was also DOA. Judging from the awkward angle of his neck and his unseeing, open eyes, he had probably gone quickly from a spinal injury.

In the third row of seats was a slightly older child, but still less than ten years old, if I had to guess. She was a mess.

I got inside the rear of the car and started work on making sure the woman was stable in case she woke and started freaking out. I had just placed a neck brace on her when it happened. I glanced up; saw her eyes, and where she was looking. She saw the dead kid beside me. That was when the screaming started, and my heart lurched inside my chest.

"HEY SURFER-MAN, why don't you follow me out, and I'll buy you a beer. Think you more than earned it on that last call," Smoke called out to me as he nodded to my Triumph. I rolled my eyes at the surfer-man reference. They'd all taken to calling me that at the station since I was from So-Cal, had long, wavy, sun-bleached blond hair, and took care of myself enough that I was ripped all over. The fact that I had never actually taken up surfing in all the time I'd lived in Cali was lost on them.

I gave a chin-tip style nod to Smoke as I threw a leg over my baby, and started her up, feeling the engine warm up to a rolling rumble beneath me. Damn, but I loved my bike. It was the one thing I'd done for myself since getting together with Kayla, and wouldn't you know it, it was also the thing she bitched about most when she wanted to spend money we didn't have. She'd talk about how I didn't need the bike since I had a truck already, and how it was wasteful.

She sure did like the few times I put her on the back and took her for a ride though. Damn woman had an orgasm just from the vibrations the first time she went out. Feeling her shudder as she straddled my hips on the bike, tits pressed into my back, was one of the reasons I forgave her bullshit bitching. Kayla may have been super high maintenance, but she put it to good use with her body too and was up for most things I suggested. The sex was both the balance and her bargaining chip. The bargaining chip part was where it became difficult to deal with.

I tried putting her, and our problems, out of my mind. Instead, I thought about how the woman from tonight's accident was going to cope with losing her husband and two of her children. My gut was still doing that twisting pit of despair move it pulled whenever something big was coming to my life, so I knew the accident wasn't the sum of what was happening. I also knew I was going to check on Beth and her daughter tomorrow, so I was going to have to keep the drinking light tonight. At least that was the plan before I saw an out and out street brawl taking place in the parking lot we were rolling into.

As we parked, and both killed our bikes, Smoke grinned over at me. "Looks like the boys are in good form tonight. Should help take your mind off shit!"

We dismounted our bikes and I followed Smoke. We passed the four guys who were rolling around on the asphalt patch beating the crap out of one another. Once inside it almost appeared as though we'd stepped into an old mountain town bar. Stone floor to ceiling pilings were interspersed down the center of the room on two sides making a central walkway that separated different areas of the large, otherwise, open space.

In the far back, stretching the length of the wall was a

wooden bar with a mirrored wall behind it; helping to give the illusion that the place was far larger than it first appeared. To my immediate right were dartboards and tables on a raised level, about two feet higher than the rest of the place. To my left were a bunch of couches and chairs thrown together with disregard for matching or usage. It looked like they'd once formed an almost circular gathering spot to make conversation easier, but they were just haphazardly strewn about instead.

A man sitting in the chair furthest from the door was getting a blowjob from a faceless blond. I meant faceless in that way that all I could see was her hair as she was bobbing her head up and down in his lap.

"Well, shit!" I commented as Smoke continued to grin and then he waved me deeper into the room, towards the bar I'd already clocked in back. Between the couch area and the bar were a few pool tables, and there were more than a few people hanging around playing, shooting the shit, and just taking up space.

Smoke ordered us both a couple beers and turned to look at me. He tipped his head toward the man receiving the blow job action in the back. "Some of the guys have no qualms about the exhibitionism. My best advice, if it bothers you, look the other way." He snatched his freshly opened bottle off the bar and tipped it in my direction before taking a sip.

I treated my beer likewise and then answered his unasked question. "Not my cup of tea but doesn't bother me either."

He nodded his head and appeared to people watch for a bit. "Hell of a bike you got outside," he finally commented.

I nodded in agreement. "She's my baby. Seems most of the guys here ride Harley, but I when saw that Triumph, and took her for a spin, I knew she was destined to by mine." I grinned at him.

"Freedom's freedom, man. Doesn't matter what label she wears so long as she gets you there," Smoke informed me.

"So fuckin' true, dude!"

"There's that surfer-man," he laughed. "Your bike's a factory custom ride, yeah?"

I tipped my head up in acknowledgment. "Yeah man, worth the extra bread too, because she's a dream to ride."

"I fuckin' bet," he offered. When I gave him a curious look, he chuckled. "Thought about snagging one, myself. I was looking at a tricked out Speedmaster a couple years ago. Wasn't factory done, just a guy who likes to tinker, and does it well." I nodded my head because I'd run into a guy once who could turn a simple bike into a work of art. I couldn't come close to affording his version of a custom ride though. That shit was far more outrageous than the nearly thirty thousand I'd spent on mine.

"Dude, you can't just leave that hanging. Why didn't you follow through?"

"Had a woman at the time that liked to use the whole, 'we'll never have kids at this rate if you keep spending all the money on that crap,' argument my way." He grinned at me then. "Saw your girl with you on the back of your ride the other day. She didn't have shit to say about yours?"

"Plenty, but the way she likes to run through money like it's water and she's dying of thirst in a desert, she couldn't really argue with me. Besides, we live together, but ain't married or even engaged, so she honestly doesn't get a say."

"Sounds healthy," he offered on a chuckle before hitting the bottle again. "You gonna put a ring on it?"

I laughed and shook my head no, vehemently.

"Too much of a pussy?"

"Fuck me!" I shouted back, nearly spewing the swig of beer I'd taken as I choked and laughed. "You could have waited until I swallowed before saying that." I told him.

"Sure thing, darlin'" a sweet little slip of a woman said as she bounced up like I'd been talking to her. I hadn't even noticed her approach. That was a feat, because it had to be damn hard to be stealthy when packing tits so large on such a petite little frame. Her bottle-blonde hair had some dark roots peeking out near her scalp, and her makeup was a bit overdone for my liking. Her clothing was too revealing as well making her look cheap rather than sexy. No way in hell would I want my woman parading around in front of all these men looking like that. Hell, a few of them were already salivating in her direction.

She lifted a hand and grabbed hold of the elastic band holding my hair back in a loose ponytail at the nape of neck. "Oh my! Look at all those curls!" The words were spoken in what was supposed to be a breathy-sexy whisper; only she had to do it louder to combat the music pumping through the speaker system. I caught her hand as she went to pull away, snatched the band from her fingers and shook my head no.

"I have a woman, and she would not appreciate someone else touching what was hers." I had no clue how Kayla would react. When we first got together, she pulled the jealous card a few times when other women checked me out or were blatant enough to hit on me in front of her, but when she realized it only made me angry for her to behave the way she had stopped doing it. It also did not matter that I wasn't planning to stay with Kayla. Until we were officially done, I would remain faithful. That was more for my peace of mind than hers, but my loyalty had always been non-negotiable.

"She's not here, is she?" The woman asked slyly with a wink as she glanced around for a strange woman who might be with me.

"No, she isn't. I don't fuck around on my woman whether I'm capable of getting away with it or not, so back off. There's plenty of men here watching you right now, so I'm sure you'll find yourself another source of entertainment with no trouble."

Her lips poked out in a good imitation of a Kayla pout, that's to say, fake as hell. Smoke laughed, clapped me on my back and then turned his back to the room. I noted he stayed vigilantly watchful using the mirrored wall in front of him though. I did not turn fully around, not liking the feeling of having my back to any doors. I did angle myself more toward Smoke though; in doing so I closed myself off to others who might attempt to approach me. Then, I took the elastic band in my hand and wound my hair up into a messy man-bun. Smoke grinned, shook his head, and then tipped it back in laughter.

"Yup, surfer-man was a good call by the guys down at the station. You're rockin' a fuckin' man bun, dude!" He teased. I just grinned back, all cocky swagger, because I knew something that made his torment meaningless. The ladies fuckin' loved the man bun. I might not have been down for cheating but seeing appreciative glances thrown my way never hurt the ego. Besides, I had rocked the short high and tight while I was in the military, and I wanted those days behind me for good.

"You ever considered joining an MC?" Smoke asked as another man, older with piercing, turquoise-colored eyes and long, dirty-blond hair, sat down on my other side.

"Had an Army buddy try to convince me to head up the west coast to Oregon to be in his club when he got back state side the last time."

"You didn't want that life?" Smoke questioned. While the other man hadn't said anything, I knew from his body language that he was paying close attention.

"Nothing to do with it. I had hooked up with a woman who had me by the dick and was not so inclined to move to the "sticks" as she called it." I laughed thinking about our recent change in scenery.

"Now you live in the actual sticks, so I assume you're no longer with her?"

"Still with her," I laughed. "She inherited a house here and I guess some money to go with it eventually. She has to live in it a year before the money gets freed up."

"You guys planning on leaving once that's settled?"

I shrugged my shoulders. "That had been the plan to start, but I'm liking it here. I fuckin' love everyone at the station. This group is so much more cohesive than the mess I had to deal with back in San Diego. I'd stay for the job alone, no shit."

Smoke's grin was back again. "Yeah, we do have a pretty tight unit there. You're lucky old Randy Cooper retired when he did and opened your spot."

"I have no doubts about that."

"If you're gonna stick around, you should stop in and hang out a bit at the club. I'll let you know when we have barbecues, parties, and the like where hang-arounds are welcome. Take advantage of it, and we'll call it testing the waters to see if this is up your alley or not."

"Yeah, man, that'd be great. Always good to be around people with similar interests."

"We have a lot of former military here too, so that helps, when shit gets all messed up in here," he tapped the side of his head and gave me a knowing look. Shit like tonight too," he added before taking another sip of his beer.

"What went down tonight?" The man sitting on my other side finally spoke up to ask Smoke.

"Accident out on the highway. Nasty business. Fuckin drunk took out a family. Woman and toddler survived, they lost the dad and two other kids that were both under ten."

"Shit!" The man beside me hissed out. "You there too?" he asked of me.

I nodded as I sipped my beer.

"Gray's our new EMT. The man is shit-hot out there in a clinch. He didn't hesitate, dove right in, got to work, dealt with the hysterical woman after she came to while trapped in their car with eyes on her dead husband and one of her dead kids. Never seen someone keep their shit together under pressure so well in my life."

"That so?" The man beside me asked, eyeing me a little more closely now. "You a vet?"

"Army Combat Medical Specialist," I informed him. He nodded.

"You serve in the sandbox?"

"Two tours before I cleared out for good," I informed him.

"Any particular reason you got out?"

"Wasn't in it for the career. I got my education, my experience, and was ready to live the good life as a civilian."

He laughed at that. "You're tied down to a crazy schedule like Smoke here, I don't exactly call that the good life, son."

"It's all about perspective. I don't have to pack a bag and be ready to go down range at a moment's notice anymore. I'm not being sent halfway around the world to take lives while trying to save them. Now, I just go do my twenty-four hours on then rest a few days before I start all over again. It works for me, especially when I have the time to hop on the bike and cruise for a bit."

"Now, you're talkin'." He held out a hand to me, and I turned so that I could address him without looking over my shoulder. "Name's Ghost. Smoke invited you to come hang out and see if you like the atmosphere, and I'm gonna second that opinion. Bring your woman along too. Lord knows they end up making the fuckin' decisions when you have an old lady."

I knew the term old lady from my buddy, and I just smirked. He was right. Kayla had been the reason I turned down the first club that tried to recruit me, after all.

I finished my beer; hung out, shot the shit with Smoke,

Ghost, and an old Vietnam Vet named Hopper after a while. I was definitely ready to take them up on the offer to come test the waters a bit more before I gave a solid yay or nay to the club life. I knew I had someone to go check on in the morning though, so I made my excuses and took off after about an hour.

Kayla was already asleep when I got home, and I didn't bother waking her. I just grabbed a shower, and climbed into bed, dog-tired as one of the guys down at the station called it.

A couple hours later, I was reminded of how bad things had been when I first got out of the Army. The last thing I remember of the dream that had woken me was a woman's bugged out eyes, blood dripping down from her temple, and the ungodly scream she let loose when she looked into the flat dead eyes of her five-year-old little boy. My heart was hammering, body covered in a cold sweat, and I was gasping for breath as Kayla rolled over and asked if I was okay.

I was not okay. I also didn't feel like sharing that with her anymore.

3. TESTING THE WATERS

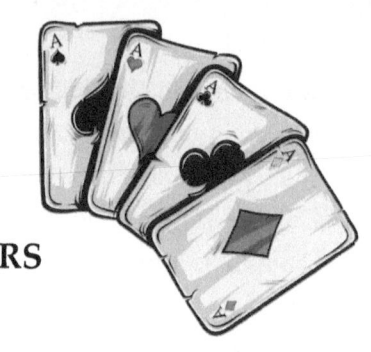

Two months after first being introduced to the dudes in Aces High, we were invited back again for a family barbecue of some sort. It hadn't been the only event we'd attended in those two months, and I was happy to see that Kayla seemed to enjoy being around the bikers and their families. She even seemed to admire the old ladies she had met, which I supposed was a good thing if I ever thought seriously about prospecting and patching in with them. She didn't even act concerned about the fact that the guys wore the one percent patches on their kuttes.

I was guessing she hadn't failed to notice the amount of money all the guys seemed to have to throw around, especially at their women. Even knowing that she noticed that, I couldn't help second guessing my decision to leave Kayla since she had been a lot better about things over the course of the two months since the accident where I met Beth and her daughter.

Once Kayla had realized what my ongoing nightmares were about, she decided to go with me one of the times I went to see Beth. She was in physical therapy by that point, working on getting full use of her leg back after being damaged in the accident. Kayla sat with me through the trial of the man who had decimated Beth's family too. He was currently behind bars serving a minimum of fifteen years for vehicular homicide for each person he killed. Sadly, the judge allowed him to serve those sentences concurrently.

I watched Kayla interacting with one of the club's women when Smoke, Ghost, and Hopper sat down around me. "How's everything going?" Ghost asked while the other two just sat and waited.

"It's all going great."

"Heard about the sentencing. That asshole needed to go down hard for what he did to that family," Ghost lamented. I found out not long ago that he had lost his wife to a car accident. I imagined my talking about Beth and her daughter all the time had to hit him hard since there was a woman currently living his history, only worse because she lost kids in the accident too.

"Agreed," I grumbled before sipping my beer and watching the three men warily. There was a cloud of tension around them that I couldn't place, and it had me sitting on edge, though I tried to keep it from notice.

"We wanted to talk to you about the state of things," Hopper finally spoke up.

"The state of things?" I questioned.

He nodded, but it was Ghost who spoke up next after

tipping his head toward Kayla. "Your woman seems to have taken a shine to the life, and you fit in well here." I nodded my agreement to both statements. "We'd like to extend an official offer for you to prospect with the club."

I couldn't hold back my emotions that well, so the grin that threatened to spread across my face bloomed right there in front of them. "That's awesome, dude. I know prospecting takes a bit of time to get through and takes up a lot of time on a daily basis as well. With me working at fire and rescue..." I started, but Smoke held up his hand to stave off my question.

"We know what your schedule is like, and it helps your case that you have a career. We'll work around your hours. When you're not there, you'll be here for the most part. Obviously, we're not talking twenty-four hours a day, seven days a week. We know you need time with Kayla too and getting your house straightened out, but prospecting will be time consuming. Kayla is welcome to come hang around when you're here so long as she isn't interfering with your duties." He gave me a knowing look before continuing. "And if you find you don't want her hanging around so much, you can always tell her to stay away, because we have club business."

That made me laugh. I'd confided in Smoke about my feelings for Kayla, and how I'd been ready to leave her a couple months ago. Hell, I was still on the fence about it. "Dude, I hear that!" I laughed out. "I'm in," I informed them as I looked at each man in turn. They all smiled openly at me. "When do I start?" Ghost had signaled someone while I was talking, and the man walked over to us and handed him what appeared to be a black leather kutte.

"Seems like now is as good a time as any," Ghost told me as he signaled for me to stand up. He came around the picnic table and stretched out the hand holding the leather. "This is yours. From the moment you take it into your hands you guard it with your life, just as you would a club brother, because it is the symbol of our club and your loyalty to it. When the time comes the prospect rocker on the back will be removed and a Cedar Falls rocker will be put in its place.

You'll also get a name patch sewn in on the front when we decide what to call you beyond prospect. As of now, that is your name here. Someone yells, 'Prospect' you come running. You do as you're told. You prove your worth, work ethic, and ability to do what is asked of you while keeping your mouth shut, and the official patches will be yours along with all the perks and promises we make as brothers and as a club."

My hand snaked out to reverently run across the leather still sitting in Ghost's arms. Holy shit! I was doing this. I was becoming a member of another brotherhood, and now I might get the chance to feel as though I belonged some-where again, for the first time since I left the Army.

"Stop molesting the damn thing, and take it already," Smoke called out to a round of laughter. It was then that I realized we had a widespread audience. Everyone had stopped what they were doing to watch as I took the kutte and put it on over the plain black t-shirt I'd worn that day.

"Fuck, dude, heavier than I thought it'd be." The words were spoken low, but Ghost heard me loud and clear.

"That's the weight of the brotherhood resting on your shoulders," he told me just as quietly as he clapped a hand to my shoulder and squeezed a moment before letting go and calling out to everyone. "Let's give our newest prospect a night to remember, because tomorrow the shit details start, and he's going to need the memories to get him through!" They all laughed, because they'd all been there and knew the score.

Smoke approached and clapped me on the shoulder in much the same way Ghost just had. "Welcome to the brotherhood man, because I have no doubts, you'll make it all the way." I nodded to him, trying to hold in the emotion that wanted to bubble up. Obviously, it wouldn't do to get fuckin' misty-eyed about belonging to something again right there in front of a yard full of bikers.

I stood there as Hopper came up with the same gesture, clapping my shoulder, a welcoming sentiment, the squeeze, and then he moved on so the next brother could take his place. They all came and welcomed me. A few promised to make my life hell over the coming months, and while they said it in good fun the glint in their eyes told me they also weren't lying. I wasn't blind. I had seen how the prospects were treated. They weren't abused in any physical manner, but they were workhorses for the club, and took their fair share of verbal abuse along the way. Prospecting was hazing at its best.

Several shots were handed to me, but before I could even get the second one down Kayla was by my side, hugging onto my middle.

"You did it! You're going to be a member soon. I'm thinking if you work hard, it won't take long, and we'll be able to have some status here, not to mention you'll be pulling in your share of the club take that the women keep telling me about." I could see the gleam in her eyes as she mentioned the money. It brought back all my doubts about her.

Kayla wasn't with me for how she felt; it was more about what I could do for her. I glanced over at Smoke, who had been in earshot of her comment, and he just shook his head back and forth a moment before giving me a look that said, 'you already knew this' and then he walked off. I did know. I thought she was changing, but now everything was clouded up again, and all it took was one fucking sentence to throw everything out of whack.

Instead of dealing with it like I should, I snatched up one of the shots that had been lined up in front of me and took it, letting out a hiss at the end, because that had been straight vodka and not the good kind.

"Dude, someone's trying to fuckin' poison me before I can have one official day of prospecting," I lamented out loud to a round of loud, ruckus laughter.

"Trial by rot-gut," one of the older guys – Tuck, I think – called out. "You survive the night with that fire in your belly, you're fit to prospect." More laughter rang out with his words, and more shots were passed my way. I wasn't a big drinker. A few beers here and there were my thing. This was going to hurt in the morning, and I didn't think the guys were going to go easy on me tomorrow when they started handing out duties.

I lost track of Kayla sometime in the night after she went

off to celebrate with some of the women. Sadly, I think she got along better with the few women who were invited to the club as entertainment than she did the actual old ladies of members. Most of the old ladies left as the night went on. More shots and drinks were delivered to me each time I was found with my hand empty. I don't know when things started to blur and become heavy, but I didn't remember much after the room started spinning and I had the fleeting memory of the question, 'how did I get inside?' before everything went dark, and nothing existed.

I woke the next morning to the world still spinning and my guts revolting against me in the worst way. Looking around, I had no clue where I was, or for that matter where the nearest bathroom was; so, I glanced around quickly and located a trashcan just to the right of the bed. I made it without a moment to spare before I threw up everything that had been on my stomach before I passed out. I had never in my life been so drunk that I passed out, never been so drunk the room was still spinning when I woke, and certainly never to the point where I had to hunt down an emergency can to puke in.

"Fuck!" The word rumbled from somewhere deep inside me as I flipped onto my back in the strange bed.

Once again, I began trying to assess my situation. I was in a strange bed, not at the house I shared with Kayla. That couldn't be good. Glancing around, I noted there wasn't any evidence that I had been in this room with anyone else. That was a relief, at least. I might be on the fence where Kayla and I staying together was concerned, but I sure as fuck was never one to cheat.

"Rise and shine, surfer-boy!" A boisterous voice called out as the door to the room I was in was flung open. I groaned loudly at the sound as the door banged into the doorstop on the wall and then bounced back only to be kicked and held open again by Smoke's booted foot. Smoke took in the stench of the room and the most likely gray pallor I had to be rocking this morning and grimaced.

"Damn shame about your condition, Prospect, because it's time to get up and get to work. Last night's party mess waits for no man."

I scrubbed my hand down across the heavy stubble lining my jaw this morning. "Where the fuck am I?"

"Clubhouse. We have rooms for guests, which don't usually include prospects, but we made an exception for your lightweight ass."

"Kayla?" I asked.

He shrugged. "Took off sometime last night with one of the girls when she realized you wouldn't be capable of driving home."

"So, she just left me here?"

He nodded. "I let her know I'd see to your ass, but she was already on her way out the door at that point. Man, I'm telling you, that woman..." he shook his head again. "I don't usually get involved in other people's shit, but are you sure you want to stick that out?"

I shook my head slowly so as not to induce any more tilt-o-whirl action in the room. "Not at all," I managed to get out before the acid burning up from my stomach rolled right into me heaving into the trash can again despite my best efforts to keep it from happening. Smoke cringed visibly as I heaved nothing but bile and regrets into the can then leaned back again on another moan.

"First duty as prospect is to get this room, and definitely that trash can cleaned up. You have fifteen minutes. Get dressed, rinse your mouth, get this shit hole smelling lemon fresh instead of puketastic, and then get your ass out to the main room for your list of shit to do. Welcome to prospecting 101, Surfer!"

"Dude," I called out in one long drawn-out word as the arm I had thrown over my face shielded me from the brightness of the room's overhead light. "I've never fuckin' surfed a day in my life."

Smoke chuckled at my admission. "That's bogus, man!" He was laughing as he closed the door on his way out.

"I never say bogus, asshole!" I shouted to the closed door. Of course, I immediately regretted shouting as my head set to throbbing all over again. "Damn!" I'd never been one to bitch and moan about my circumstances so instead I got up, found another door in the room that apparently led to a bathroom – which would have been nice to know about twenty minutes ago – and took my can in there to wash it out.

Once I was done with the dirty deeds the room required to be refreshed, I took a few minutes to splash some water on my face, rinse my mouth, and pray for time to take a shower at some point in the day. I stunk to high heaven with the amount of alcohol fumes seeping from my pores. I wished I had access to my rig right about now, because the best thing to cure a hangover was hydration, and a quick infusion of liquids into my system through an

IV would be just the ticket. I'd done it for plenty of guys during my time in the Army, but it looked like I was just everyone else's hangover savior. My dumbass was going to have to trudge through the day hydrating the old-fashioned way.

"Prospect!" Hopper yelled as I made my not so grand, slump-shouldered entrance into the main room. "You get that room clean? Smoke said you stunk it up good and proper and managed to yak in the trashcan too." All of this was said good in a natured way, even if overly loud in delivery.

"S'all good," I managed to mumble.

"Right then," he stated as he hopped down off the stool he'd been seated on. "First order of business is getting all the trash off the lawn from last night." He led me to the back door and all but pushed my sluggish body outside. He did, at least, hand me a bottle of water as I was shoved onto the multi-level back deck. It looked like no one in this whole damn place new what a trashcan was for. There were left over plates, beer cans, bottles, and fuckin' condoms – not empty – all over the damn place.

"The guys can be some seriously nasty bastards, especially when a new prospect is chosen," one of the other prospects for the MC stated as he too glanced over the fresh hell we'd been pushed into this morning.

"Fuck!" That was pretty much all I had the energy to say. "We have gloves or some shit? I'm not picking up nasty fuckin' condoms with my bare hands." The kid beside me frowned, and then shook his head back and forth slowly as if just realizing it was going to be down to one of us to do just that. "Right, then we're just going to have to get creative. Use the plates to scoop them up and pray like hell nothing spills out in the process."

I was off to work as the kid stood there turning green behind the gills. The one leg up I had in this was that I wasn't squeamish. My job required an iron stomach. I'd seen a lot in my years of working as a battlefield medic, but I'd seen the lowest, most disturbing aspects of humanity on the job with EMS over the years. You do not want to know the kinds of shit people stick in orifices that weren't meant to house those things. I shook off the thought before my hangover weakened stomach called me out as a liar today. Damn all those shots straight to hell!

It took the two of us damn near three hours to clean up the mess just on the outside of the clubhouse. It probably would have gone quicker if the wind hadn't decided to go from stagnant to summer breeze worthy blowing all the loose plates, napkins, and other questionable shit all over the fucking yard. Some of the guys even came out and placed bets on whether the wind would win in scooping away the mess before we managed to chase it down. Of course, we weren't really in danger of the wind winning in that regard, because there was a damn ten-foot-tall privacy fence surrounding the entire property. That didn't mean the wind didn't blow that shit hell and far gone from where most of the mess had been located on the deck.

Day one of prospecting sucked balls, but I was no quitter, so the job got done. The other prospect hadn't quit either, but he also hadn't exactly been energetic in getting shit done. He was the other reason we got finished so slowly. I'm not a big fan of having to pick up other people's slack, so I took the lead, even as he bitched and complained that he had seniority since he'd been prospecting for four months already.

"Yeah, well, guess what, kid?"

"They call me Mouth," he stated angrily, clearly not like being called kid.

"Guess what kid?" I asked again, because fuck him. "Your four months don't mean shit to me when you don't take charge and get shit done on your own. Now, get the lead out of your ass and let's get this finished, because I'm hungry, tired, and hung over. The longer this takes, the longer I go without food. The longer I go without food, the worse I am to deal with, you feel, dude?"

"Whatever, man!" The guy mumbled. He seriously couldn't have been more than nineteen, and I honestly wasn't certain why they would have chosen him to prospect in the first place. He did not strike me as a go-getter. Then again, I supposed you didn't really need to be in an MC. You just had to be loyal. Although, his bitching attitude explained why he already had the name Mouth.

Two other prospects were due in that evening to take over for Mouth and me. I had to work the next day, so Smoke made sure the guys knew I needed my rest before shift started. Considering rest mattered in whether I did my job well or not, and that job was literally life or death sometimes, they didn't give me any shit about it. Mouth, however, gave me plenty of shit.

"Why the fuck are *you* so special?" He had asked me when the guys told him he had to stay after I was dismissed. I didn't get to answer, because Ghost beat me to it.

"He gets to leave because he has an important job to get to tomorrow in the real world, and he didn't fuck around here today. He took charge, got shit done, and didn't slack the fuck off. Maybe, you should pay attention to the new guy and how he operates and see how to make life easier on yourself."

The kid's face had burned into several different shades of red as he ground his teeth so hard to fight back his own temper that I knew he must be doing damage to his teeth or jaw. I didn't stick around to see how that played out, because I was still starving, and I honesty wasn't sure if I had the energy to even bother fixing that issue at this point, because my body was ready to give out.

I got on my bike, headed to the diner to nab a bite, and then went home to see that Kayla had the house destroyed. Apparently, she had taken the party home with her the night before and didn't bother cleaning up. It was like walking onto the club's deck this morning all over again. Only this time it was my living room.

"Kayla, what the fuck?" I yelled as she stumbled out of the bedroom looking completely wrecked and holding on to her head.

"Shh," she hissed. "My head is killing me!"

"Why the fuck does our house look worse than the club-house did this morning?"

She glared in my direction then looked around the living room and winced. "The girls and I left the clubhouse and came here last night."

"Yeah? I've spent all day getting the clubhouse straight-ened up, why haven't you cleaned this shit up yet?"

She stared at me, mouth agape. "What was I supposed to do? Most of it isn't my mess."

"And?"

"And what? Why should I be responsible for cleaning it when most of it wasn't my mess?" she shouted, and then winced as the sound went to her head.

"Who the fuck do you think is supposed to clean it?"

"I don't know, you?"

I laughed. She didn't.

"You're the prospect. It's your job to clean up messes left behind by club events."

"This wasn't a club event. The only club event took place at the clubhouse last night, and I did clean that shit up. Took all fuckin' day. This," I pointed at the mess all over the place. "This is your mess, and you will clean it the fuck up! You invited people over; you're responsible for the messes they make. You don't want to clean it all by yourself, you make sure they help before they bail on you." I moved to go around her toward the bedroom.

"That's not fair," she whined.

"Oh? But it's fair that I have to clean up after a party I didn't even attend when I was up cleaning and hung over all day at the clubhouse, and have to work a twenty-four-hour shift tomorrow?"

"I... You don't get it..." she huffed.

"Nope, I sure as fuck do not. Get this shit cleaned up, Kay, because I'm not fuckin' doing it."

Two hours later, my nap was disturbed by Kayla's shouting. "You're not working fast enough!" I walked out into the living room to find her sitting on the couch, flipping through something on her phone, and a sweet older lady was standing there glaring at her with a trash bag in her hands.

"You didn't say the job would be this big or I would have brought help, and the quote I gave you for cleaning three rooms of the house did not cover cleaning up after a major party. There are specific charges for that, and it takes more time."

"Oh no! You are not going to fleece me out of more money just because you're too lazy to work faster."

"Kayla!" I shouted causing both women to jump and turn to look at me as I stood there in nothing but boxer briefs and the frown that was becoming a permanent fixture on my face. "What in the absolute fuck is going on here?"

"Um," she started, but I held up my hand in the air to silence her bullshit.

"How much did she pay you for your services?" I questioned the woman.

"She hasn't paid me yet, but I told her it would be $75 for the three rooms. That was before I saw the condition that they were in. She didn't inform me that there had been a party here. My website says specifically that there are different rates for that," the woman tacked on as she turned her glare back in Kayla's direction.

I glanced around and noted the room was about half done. "One moment," I held a finger up as I went back to the room to grab my wallet. I snagged $75 out of it and handed it to the woman. "That should cover what you've already done. Thank you, and if she ever calls again, just tell her no." The woman grinned, gathered her things, and left.

"What did you do that for? She wasn't done cleaning."

"I told you to clean up your own fuckin' mess. I meant it." I turned to go back to the room, but added, "And you owe me $75."

"How about I take it out of your rent?" she asked snidely. Since there wasn't a mortgage on the house there wasn't any rent due.

"How about I start calculating all the work and money I've put into the house and property and put a lien on the house for the amount owed back to me, and we can fight it out in court if that's how you want to be? Maybe, instead of all that noise you could just try taking responsibility for yourself and your actions for once, Kay, because I gotta tell you, this shit is getting old as fuck!"

I'd like to think I was getting through to her when I saw the momentary panic in her eyes, but I knew better. She might play nice today, and get her shit together momentarily, but it would never last. She'd proven that by having the night she did and expecting me to be the one to clean up after her.

"I'm sorry, I'm just bitchy, because this hang over is epic."

"You think mine isn't?" She looked at me blankly and completely missed the point. "Mine was hard to deal with all day, but I dealt. You need to start learning to deal with real life and not the fantasy you lived with as a child. You're not a child, and you were cut off from that life. At some point, you need to grow up and start living in the life you have. If you don't like it, find a way to make it better, but don't expect everyone else in the world to do it for you. That's not how shit works, Kay."

Again, she just stared, and I wondered if anything I ever said to her got through. Instead of commenting she just turned on her heels and walked away, once again leaving the mess she made behind. I had work to get to in the morning so instead of worrying about it I left the mess, forgot about Kayla, got a shower, and went back to bed.

4. FUNDRAISER

THE NEXT TWO MONTHS OF PROSPECTING WENT JUST ABOUT THE same, minus the shots from the first night. I was a slave to the club three days out the week, had one off to myself, and the other three were spent working at the station and saving lives. Kayla was a mixed bag. Some days weren't as bad as others, but her party messes on the days I would come home from work or from prospecting duties started to become a problem. I let them slide since I was hardly there to deal with any of it, and Smoke was kind enough to let me store all of my important shit at his house, just in case one of the people Kay had around was up to no good.

The things I had been doing with my days off was what had me at the clubhouse today. I had been going to see Beth and Abby, the woman and child who survived the car wreck the night I was asked to think about joining the MC. They were doing okay, struggling a bit without the rest of their family though, which was why I showed up to see if Beth needed anything done that her husband used to do.

Some days I found myself doing the lawn, once I was unclogging a sink, another time I took care of Abby while her mom did physical therapy. Yesterday, I had walked into Beth sobbing over bills. There were medical bills, bills from the funeral home, and then her normal household bills sitting piled up along with a calculator, a sheet of paper, and a bunch of scribbled out numbers.

Ghost noticed me when I walked in the clubhouse after coming from seeing Beth and he did a double take before he tipped his chin up at me. "What can we do for you today, or did you decide to sign on for another round of abuse from the guys on your day off?"

I shook my head and the look on my face must have tipped him off to the serious nature of my visit. "Please, tell me you haven't come to quit on us," he huffed out which made me smile.

"Nah, nothing like that. I do have a favor to ask of the club though, and I don't know if I have the right to do that since I'm only a prospect, but it's important."

"Come back to my office, let's talk." Ghost led me down a hallway lined with photos taken throughout the years of club members, their families, and tons of bikes. The walls back here were like a time capsule keeping the history of the club alive for everyone. Once we ducked into Ghost's office, he motioned for me to have a seat on the leather couch under the barred window. "Have a seat and tell me what's on your mind."

"The first night we met here," I started. Ghost appeared lost in thought for a moment, and then nodded his head for me to continue. "Smoke and I had worked a pretty nasty accident that night."

"Drunk driver, woman lost her husband and two kids, right?" he asked.

I nodded. "Beth," I informed him. "I've been spending my days off going over to help her out. It's just her and her little girl, Abby now; and there's no one to do all the things her husband used to."

Ghost cocked his head to the side and looked at me a little differently then. "That's... Shit, I want to say that is a fuckin' great thing you're doing, but I'm pretty sure you're trained not to get that involved. You can't help all the people you'll treat over the years."

"No, but every once in a while, there's a special case. I dream of that accident still, and it has been months. I can't imagine what it was like for Beth. Seeing her kid, and her husband, then waking up in the hospital to find out what really happened, and all she lost." I shuddered, and it manifested physically. "Anyway, I go there and mow the lawn, fix the plumbing, the shit the man of the house usually takes care of. You know?"

Ghost again tipped his head. "You're not getting involved with her in a romantic way, are you?" It was a legitimate enough question.

"No. No way. Beth is a sweet lady, but it's not like that. She's just drowning man. There's a lot going on with her physical therapy, caring for her daughter who still doesn't grasp that her siblings and dad aren't coming back, you know how it is."

"I do," Ghost informed me, and I remembered hearing

stories about the wife he had lost, and then the years he had lost with his own daughter as a result of how he chose to deal with his grief.

"Well, when I went by yesterday, Beth had all these bills strewn about across the table. Medical, funeral, household stuff, it all added up to a fuck of a lot. She said her husband's life insurance only paid out $30,000. He had canceled the other policy they had because they couldn't afford it at the time. It was the one that would have covered the rest of the mortgage and whatnot. She used it to get out from under the car payment and what she could of the mortgage. She paid most of the funeral expenses, but not all since there were three people to have buried. There's nothing left, and the drunk that hit her didn't have insurance, the family only had the minimum required by law, because of things being tight with money.

Anyway, she owes a shit ton of money, and her health insurance got cut off this month. It had been extended, but she can't afford the payouts to keep it any longer, which is where the rest of that 30k went. I helped get her set up with an interview to apply for Medicaid, but until it goes through, she's just kind of stuck."

"I get that. Where is all this going as far as the club is concerned?"

"I was hoping that you could talk the guys into doing a fundraiser, maybe a poker run or something like that, to raise money for Beth and her daughter to help them get back on their feet. It's not fair that this woman lost most of her family in one accident, and she's having to stress daily over how to feed her daughter and pay these bills that are looming." I sighed as I took in Ghost's blank expression. "I'll help with whatever I can. I'll take time off work to organize it, work it, do whatever I can to take as much of the burden off the club as possible, but I obviously can't do it all on my own."

Ghost held his hand up to me. "Son, I gotta tell you, from the moment we met I had a feeling about you. Hearing Smoke praise you the way he did about that night, well, it kind of cemented that feeling I got. I cannot express how much what you're asking of the club has me questioning my initial assessment of you."

Fuck, what the hell did that mean? Had I asked too much of them while still being a prospect? "I just thought..." I started to say, but he cut me off again.

"I don't think you're understanding what I'm putting out there. You have blown away my expectations from day one, Gray. Blown them away completely, and you continue to do so. We need more men in the club who think like you. You're quick on your feet, intelligent, watchful, and fuckin' compassionate. Compassion is missing in a lot of the shit we do, so it humbles me when one of my men brings it to the table as a matter of importance. You want a fun run to make money for Beth and her girl? We will make it happen. I'll get the guys into church later today, and we'll discuss logistics and see how quickly we can put shit together. No need in that woman stressing any longer than she has to."

I leaned my head back on the couch and let the breath I'd been holding blow out harshly. The tension in my shoulders released with the knowledge that I had good men at my back who were willing to step up and help me help someone else.

"I can't tell you how fuckin' grateful I am, dude. That's just... Fuck! Thank you!" I attempted to swallow back the knot of emotion lodged in my throat as I lifted my head and glanced back over at Ghost.

"Wish that I had someone with your heart around when I lost my old lady. I think you're just what I would have needed to kick my ass in gear so I wouldn't have lost my Jamie too. Beth and Abby are lucky you were the one responding that night. You make me proud, Gray. You make this club proud. We'll get shit together, and let you know how we need you to help." We both stood then as he clapped me on my shoulder and squeezed just as he had done after I donned my kutte for the first time. "Lookin' forward to the day you patch in, because I have high hopes for what you'll bring to this club."

"Thanks," I managed to get out.

"Now, get out of here and enjoy the rest of your day off before someone puts your ass to work."

"You don't have to tell me twice." At least one thing was going well in my life, and that shit was worth celebrating, so I texted Smoke on my way out to let him know we needed to go out and do just that. Unfortunately, he couldn't make it because his ass was at a hockey game in Pennsylvania of all things. The crazy ass bastard was seeing the sister of one our club brothers. I just hoped that shit worked out for him, because that was dangerous water to be treading in.

5. FUN RUN

THE CLUB MORE THAN EXCEEDED MY EXPECTATIONS WHILE PUTTING the event together to help Beth out. Aces High organized a poker run in two weeks, invited a bunch of guys from chapters out of town as well as from some of the clubs they associated with outside of Aces High. Civilians were also encouraged to join in if they had a ride. The turnout was phenomenal. I was manning a booth in the middle of town where the guys would stop to pick up their last card before heading on to the clubhouse to see who had the winning hand.

Hopper had donated a private chopper ride as part of the prizes and one of the guys donated a custom Bobber with satin black paint, black and chrome engine, and twelve-inch ape hangers. The bike was a beauty and held a certain appeal for the guys who loved the style. It certainly made the $100 per ticket buy-in for the poker run worth it to whoever won the thing. The old ladies had also set up an auction and bake sale for participants who were unable to ride but wanted to help contribute to the cause.

The town of Cedar Falls rallied as well, emptying their wallets in some seriously generous donations. Some of the donations were monetary, but others were for services like free basic maintenance on Beth's vehicle for two years. The event wasn't even halfway over, and we had already managed to raise around $35,000 in cash in addition to extra services. I was fuckin' ecstatic, and beyond grateful to everyone in the club and this little town for stepping up and getting shit done. This kind of thing wouldn't have gone half as well in my hometown and Cedar Falls was a fraction of its size and population. There was something to be said for a tight-knit community.

I glanced up from where I was organizing the table to find Beth standing there with tears in her eyes as she held Abby, who was propped on her hip and busy eating a popsicle.

"Gray," she whispered before coming around the table to wrap me in a hug that Abby joined in on, sticky fingers and all. "I don't know what to say. This is so much."

"Just wait until you see how much we've raised so far," I informed her with a wink as she swiped at a stray tear that had fallen.

"I don't know how we can ever thank you and the club."

"Just be happy, Beth. That's all we want."

She nodded her head and then glanced back over her shoulder at someone. When I tore my gaze from the girls I had been looking after I was socked in the gut by the beauty standing there smiling so brightly over at me. Auburn hair was pulled back into a strange looking braid while bright green eyes took me in from top to toe. The freckles across the bridge of her nose and cheeks stood out in the sunshine but did not distract from the complete package.

The woman was taller than Beth, though probably half a foot or more shorter than my six feet, two inches. She wore a light blue sundress, and I could just barely make out the fact that it had those thin straps holding it to her shoulders underneath the sweater she wore over top. The dress itself draped down her slender body to pool just above her sandaled feet.

"Thank God for the weather we had this weekend. Indian summers are a blessing for events like this." I cringed a little because I wasn't much for God or the bible thumping type and wouldn't that figure I meet a woman who is a stunning goddess only to be confronted by her religion.

"It is the perfect weather," I responded having enjoyed the lows in the sixties and highs topping out in the mid-seventies today. A gentle breeze blew every now and again, but there wasn't a cloud to be seen in the skies above, just a solid sheet of blue for the guys to ride under. A small part of me wished I had been able to participate in the actual run, but then again, I was happy to just have the backing of the club for this so manning the booth was worth missing the perfect riding day.

"Gray, this is my best friend in the world, Gillian Thomas, or Gillie-Bean as Abby and I call her. Gillie, this is Daniel Grayson, but everyone calls him Gray for some reason."

"That or surfer dude, surfer boy, or just plain surfer," Smoke cut in as he walked up to the booth I was manning.

"Why surfer?" Gillie asked.

I laughed. "Who knows? They've been calling me that since I first said 'dude' to them. I'm from So-Cal, so they seem to think that means I surf when you put the two together."

Gillie laughed and I swear it was like angels were crying somewhere for the beauty of the sound she made. Then I noticed the little boy that was attempting to climb my bike and I grinned over at him. "You trying to steal my bike, little dude?" I asked. Gillie gasped when she glanced over and saw what was going on.

"Kade Thomas, you get your butt off that motorcycle right now!"

I walked over to the boy. "How about we take your picture first, since you already managed to climb on up?"

"Yeah!" The boy shouted excitedly. "Mommy, take my picture. I stoled the bike, so now it's mine," he explained with a giggle.

"Well, I guess it's too bad you're going to have to give it right back to the man then, because you're not allowed to ride a motorcycle just yet."

"Aww man," the kid lamented while managing a full-on pouty face. "That sucks!"

"Kade, you don't say that something sucks," Gillie corrected, and I assumed at that point that she was his mother. I also put two and two together that her last name was the same as the kid's, and it made me wonder if she was married to his dad or if she was a single mom.

"If you want, I can take a picture for you so that you can get in there with him?" I asked her and held my hand out for her cell phone. She relinquished it to me and simply scrunched down beside the bike instead of trying to mount the thing the way her son had. I took the picture and then added my information to her phone while she dealt with getting her boy off my bike.

I texted the picture of the two of them to myself and couldn't have explained why I did it at the time, except that the woman had stunned me stupid. Her kid was not only cute, but ballsy to be climbing on a biker's ride. Apparently, his mom had warned him about touching motorcycles belonging to bikers, and the kid thought he could cute his way out of trouble with his dimpled grin.

Once his mom finished lecturing him, she stood and held her hand out for her phone. I gently placed it in the palm she had outstretched, and as I let go my fingers trailed along her palm too. The gooseflesh it produced on her arms was satisfying since it meant I wasn't the only one affected here.

"Hey, man, last biker doing the run came through about fifteen minutes ago. Figured I'd give you a hand tearing everything down here so you can get on over to the club-house for the prizes being awarded and to hear the final tally on what was raised." Smoke had been standing there the whole time, and I'd forgotten all about it. Damn.

"Thanks man, I appreciate that. I thought Mouth was supposed to come help once they shut down the first two stops, but he never showed."

"Yeah, he's not as reliable as we'd hoped. He called and said he had a personal matter to attend to and didn't bother elaborating on what that was." Smoke turned to the women and children then. "You ladies coming over to the clubhouse for the festivities?"

"Is it okay to bring the kids?" Beth asked.

"Sure, they're welcome. There will be plenty of families there today, so they won't feel out of place at all. Fair warning though, some of the guys don't always remember to sensor their language around the kids, so it's an at your own risk thing, but I promise that will be the worst of it."

"Okay, well, that shouldn't be a problem," Beth assured Smoke. "Thank you again for everything your club has done for us, and everything you and Gray did that night." She choked up on the last and I pulled her in for a hug.

"No thanks necessary, Beth. I already told you that." I noticed Gillie was smiling at me as I gave Beth a squeeze and released her. "You guys driving over together?"

"Yeah, we'll see you there soon," Beth told me as they both started gathering the kids and backing away. Smoke and I packed up the table, chairs, and the drinks that had been left before he informed me that we were just to leave the van there, locked. I had ridden my bike here earlier in the day and one of the other guys had already parked the van full of supplies by the time I'd arrived.

As we packed the last of it into the van Smoke looked me over as if seeing me for the first time. "You don't look at Kayla the way you were looking at Beth's friend."

"What are you talking about? I'm not a cheater, dude."

"Not saying you are. I'm just pointing out that if things were ever really going to work with you and Kayla, you wouldn't even have noticed little miss Gillie-Bean." With that he hopped on his bike, started her up, and drove off while I stood there contemplating those words and wondering what the hell kind of look I'd given Gillian to prompt that bit of soul stirring honesty from my friend.

Before I could get on my bike two other prospects showed up and gave me a quick chin tip as they went about securing the van and hopping in. Holden – known by everyone as Hold 'Em since he was such a lady's man – and Darryl fired the van up and took off for the clubhouse with me trailing behind them. I was more excited to get there than I should have been, and I didn't want to even begin to examine the reasons for that. I was also starting to hate Smoke for putting it out there. I had enough woman troubles as is, I certainly didn't need to add perfect chemistry with a stranger to the mix in order to confuse things even more.

An hour after arriving I still hadn't seen Beth or Gillie, and I began to worry about them. I had thought they were coming straight to the clubhouse when they left the check-in point I'd been stationed at, which happened to be the last one before the end. I had swept the clubhouse, both inside and out numerous times now and still no sight of them. "Why don't you just call and check on them?" A voice called out from just over my shoulder. I turned to see Smoke standing there with a woman I hadn't met yet.

"I think maybe I should. I thought they were coming straight here."

Smoke shrugged his shoulders. "Maybe one of the kids got cranky, it happens with my nephew sometimes, and my sister has to cancel plans or rearrange shit at the last minute." I nodded wondering if the woman standing with Smoke was his sister but judging by the way they kept touching one another in a flirty way, I was thinking not. He caught me watching them and smiled. "Surfer-man, this is Poppy. She's new around here, moved up to Cedar Falls from Georgia to be closer to her brother, Chief."

"Chief's pretty cool," I stated before turning to her. "Nice to meet you, Poppy." We shook hands as I noticed that Chief was watching Smoke and his sister from across the room with a smile on his face. I hadn't had much interaction with him yet, as he'd been out of town helping a sister with moving. I was now guessing that had been Poppy. He had been one of the club brothers feeding me shots the first night I got my kutte though.

"I better go make that call," I stated and walked away while Smoke and Poppy grinned at one another. Who knew what that shit was about?

I was standing there, dialing Beth's phone when I heard someone's phone blaring the ringtone Born to be Wild just behind me. I turned to see whom it was, and Beth was standing there holding up her phone and smiling at me. "Well, I guess you know what your ringtone is now," she offered with a shrug.

I just smiled at her. "I was just starting to get worried that I hadn't seen you guys here." He glanced around then, not seeing Gillie, Kade, or Abby. "Where is everyone else?"

"Gillie is getting us drinks from the bar, but we dropped Kade and Abby off with Kade's grandma. Abby was cranky since she missed her nap, and Gillie didn't even want to guess at what kind of trouble Kade would get into with all the bikers around. He's been in heaven watching them ride all over town all day."

"I can imagine. If I'd been involved with something like this as a boy, I would have been in heaven too," I confirmed with a grin. "Just wait until he's a teenager and comes around," I told her with a wag of my brows as hers rose in surprise. I hadn't even meant to sound like I would have a connection with Gillie and Kade that far in the future, but the words just slipped out as if it was a forgone conclusion. "I mean, you know, since he lives in a town with an MC in it, it's bound to happen at some point."

"Uh-huh," Beth hummed out with a knowing grin. It was then that both Gillie – laden with two beers – and Kayla – full of attitude – showed up at the same time.

Kayla immediately snaked a hand around my arm, claiming me as her own and giving the stink-eye to Beth. She had grown increasingly jealous and pissed off about the time I spent helping the woman out, especially when I continued to refuse to help Kayla clean up after her numerous parties. "What are you doing over here, when you should have come and found me?" Kayla asked.

"I was just talking to Beth, and you're perfectly capable of coming to me."

Kayla narrowed her eyes at me. "It's your job in this relationship to hunt me down and fetch me drinks. You're a prospect here anyway, so it's your job period. Why are you standing around talking to her when you have shit to do to impress the guys?"

I was speechless for a moment but found I didn't need to say shit because Ghost had walked up in time to hear her spout off her bullshit. "Gray here put all the cogs in motion for this shindig and worked a booth all day that I've heard you never showed up to, because you were too busy at one of the pre-parties. The women told me you didn't even bother to bring anything for the auction or bake sale, let alone help with either. Considering this was your man's event he put together, I'm seriously wondering why you – as his soon to be old lady – didn't help out with anything at all?"

"Well, I..." she started, looking around at all the people eyeing her now and growing red-faced with embarrassment. She then glanced back to me to help bail her out of the mess her mouth had just made, and when I didn't, she carried on. "I had things to do this morning, and I worked yesterday so it's not like I could bake."

"A lot of the women here worked yesterday, hell some of them had to work today, and still managed to contribute. Let me hear you talk to your man the way you just did one more time in my clubhouse and I will see you aren't welcomed back. Whether Gray still wants to show up or not when that happens will be up to him." With that, Ghost gave me a meaningful look before he wandered off again. Beth and Gillie had already slunk away into the crowd, though I noted both were still keeping an eye on the scene as they did so.

"Why in the hell did you stand there and let him embarrass me like that?" Kayla fumed at me after Ghost was no longer in earshot.

"Why the hell did you think it was okay to come to me and do the same? You're supposed to be here to support the cause, the club, and me. If you can't do those things you should leave."

"What?" she hissed out through clenched teeth.

"You heard me."

"But you've been spending all your free time with that woman and her brat. I deserve that time. I don't know why you can just up and go mow the lawn at her house, but you can't clean our house up on your day off."

"Kayla, I'm fuckin' done with this bullshit of yours. Get the fuck out of here with that shit, right fuckin' now."

"What are you saying?"

"I'm saying if you're not contributing anything more to the night than being an entitled bitch you can leave, because you aren't wanted here. This day is important, and I won't have you ruining it."

Before she could say the word, Ghost stood on one of the raised portions of the deck where the Bobber that would go to the poker run winner was sitting in pride of place. "All right everyone, first off, I want to thank our prospect, Gray for putting this little shindig together for us, in support of Beth Sayers and her daughter Abby. They lost far too much already when Beth's husband and two of her children were taken in a tragic accident involving a drunk driver. They shouldn't be left shouldering a burden that pulls them down further than grief can on its own.

"Times like these show the true character of people, and I have to say, our prospect is well on his way to becoming a brother we can all be proud of and one that we want at our sides. He's been taking care of Beth and her daughter since he helped pull her from that wreck, and I want to put it out there to Beth tonight, that he will no longer be doing that alone. You have need of anything, from a shoulder to cry on to lawn service, or anything in between, you call on us. Aces

65

High will be there to help. That is my promise today above all else that goes on here."

I took note of Beth with rivers of tears running down her cheeks as her friend pulled her into a tight side-hug. Rounds of male agreement went up around the room along with some very vocal old ladies chiming in. My chest swelled with pride to be a part of this group that would embrace a stranger I had brought into their midst. If I ever had doubts about joining an MC they were quashed in that moment.

"Now, for the announcements you've all been waiting for," Ghost yelled out as Prospect Hold 'Em handed him a clipboard with the results of the poker run. "We had 350 men and women participate in the poker run. The entry fees of $100 per person or $150 per couple added up to $24,000 for the 160 couples attending and $19,000 for the 190 single tickets that were sold. That's a total of $43,000 for just the poker run entry fees. You guys outdid yourselves, and we want to say thank you to all the participants who purchased tickets even as only 217 riders were able to show up out of the 350 tickets purchased. Every little bit counts, and we are thankful. The old ladies put on a bake sale and auction today as well earning $782 from bake sale proceeds and $4,500 from the auction. We also had a few monetary donations come in from the citizens of Cedar Falls and those totaled $6,750. The grand total for today's event was $55,032. There are also promissory notes for services here for you Beth from Timberland Lawn Care, Aces Auto Garage, and a gift certificate worth $350 for Posh Kids Clothing down on Main Street."

Ghost took note of the fact that Beth was a complete

emotional mess and smiled sweetly down at her. "We'll get it all straightened out for you with details tomorrow, sweetheart." Ghost glanced around and held the clipboard over his head then. "As for the rest of you assholes. Let's find out who won this beautiful Bobber that our Nomad, Bishop, was kind enough to donate to the cause." Ghost glanced down at the clipboard, rolled his eyes, lifted his head with a smirk planted firmly on his face. "Of course, it would be you. Fuckin' Rabbit of the Dakota Chapter, get your ass up here!"

Hooting and hollering exploded all around as a tall man with long golden-brown hair started strutting his stuff up to the top deck where Ghost stood beside the bike he'd just won. It was good to see another biker with long wavy hair like my own. "Hell yeah," Rabbit called out as he ran his hand over the ape bars. "This is one sweet fuckin' ride, but I'm afraid I have no way to get her home, and my Lulu would be devastated if I rode anyone but her." Rabbit glanced out into the crowd, pointed at Beth, and winked at her playfully. "This one is for you sweetheart!" He then held up a hand to quiet everyone down. "Since I have no way to get her home, I want to offer the Bobber up for auction with the proceeds going toward rounding out the night's take for Beth and her daughter. Serious bids only, and you bastards better be able to produce cash for her within 24 hours if you bid. Minimum opening bid is $15,000." It was actually a low-ball bid for the custom ride, but I honestly didn't think he'd get much more for it since it was an impromptu auction.

A bidding war commenced and ended at $32,500. Everyone glanced around to see who had won the bike and a lanky man wearing wire-framed glasses stepped forward to claim his prize with the biggest, goofiest grin on his face I had ever seen. It was clear the dude was not a biker, but maybe it had been a long-lost childhood dream to become one.

"And who do we have here?" Rabbit asked, obviously not knowing who the man was since he wasn't from here.

"I'm Dr. Collins. Stewart Collins. I um, I worked on Beth when she was brought into the emergency room." He looked out into the crowd then and found Beth standing there. Smoke and Poppy had moved in to stand beside her and Gillie, and Beth was leaning heavily into Smoke. "If I could have waived all the hospital fees for you, I would have. I did waive my personal fees for your surgery, but I hope this helps to ease the burden of the rest of it."

Man, I could not even begin to process the amount of love and charity this town had to give. "I just got my motorcycle endorsement a few months ago, and this bike is way better than the one I had," he announced to a ton of laughter as he lovingly stroked the leather seat of the Bobber.

"Alrighty then," Ghost shouted out. "Congrats to Doc Collins on winning the auction for the Bobber that Rabbit won, and Bishop donated before that. You're all some really charitable motherfuckers up in here today!"

More laughter ensued and helped to lighten the mood. Even Beth chuckled at that, which made me happy. "Next on the agenda is the runner up package that involves this asshole here," Ghost patted Hopper on the back. "Taking one of you unlucky shits, or a couple, up in his chopper. No, I don't mean the kind you ride bitch on. I mean he's going to fly you around for a special time. If you get too excited and make his seats messy, you best believe you'll be the ones cleaning up after yourselves."

"Fuckin' Christ!" Hopper added as he smacked his own forehead at the prospect of having someone cream all over the seats in his helicopter.

"Bender, you were the runner up in the poker run! Congrats, brother! I'm sure your old lady will be making you drag her along for that trip." Ghost laughed then looked at Hopper. "Might want to get some seat covers! With those two up there together, they might come down with another baby on board."

"Fuck that, my little man is a terror. We aren't ready, but we sure as fuck will take that ride!" Bender called out to a plethora of good-natured teasing as he went to collect the shiny certificate the guys had printed up for the winners. A few more awards were given out, including Das Boot – the glass boot full of room temperature beer – for the lowest scoring person.

"It's a good thing he's already known as Shameless, because otherwise he'd never live down that rotten ass hand of his," Ghost called out to ruckus laughter. "Get on up here and take your boot, man! You deserve it, and hell, you need to drown your sorrows after this shit show of a hand you had. Let's get Shameless a shot of something too! The boot won't be enough to come back from this."

Once the laughter over Shameless' horrific loss died down it sunk in that we had managed to raise $87,532 plus some extras for Beth and her daughter. My heart felt light and full all at the same time as I went to her and gave her a giant hug.

"I don't know how to thank you," she managed to get out through hiccups brought on by her happy tears and sobbing.

"What did I tell you before? You don't have to thank me, ever. I only do the things I want."

"Yeah, but I've obviously caused trouble with your girl-friend," she lamented, and I noticed Kayla standing off by the bar shooting daggers in our direction.

"Sweetheart trust me when I say you caused nothing. My issues with Kayla were already there before. Don't you worry about that. You enjoy the rest of your night, and the fact that some of those worries you had when I walked in a couple weeks ago are now gone."

We hugged again and I noticed Gillie watching us, her emerald eyes shining with unshed tears as she mouthed 'thank you' to me. I nodded and smiled back at her as I hugged Beth tighter. Then I went to collect my bitch of a girl-friend to get her out of there before she caused another scene, because judging by her body language she was already ramping up for it.

6. CALLED AWAY

It was my first day off from rescue, and I didn't have to be at the club until later in the evening which is why it was odd that my phone was ringing too close by to have been where I left it. I barely opened one of my eyes to peek out and noticed Kayla sitting beside me in bed staring at my phone with a look of panic like she'd just been caught red handed at something, and she had.

"Why do you have my phone, and who is calling?"

"Smoke's calling," she answered and tossed it on my chest.

I picked up the phone and answered. "Hello?"

"Hey man, sorry to wake you, but we're going to need you a bit earlier today. We have a run, last minute thing, and need a body to drive the van."

"Sure, when and where?"

Smoke offered up details and then disconnected. I had two hours to get ready and haul my ass to the clubhouse, but that didn't mean it had escaped my notice that Kayla hadn't answered what she'd been doing with my phone. I immediately flipped to my texts and saw she had sent out a message to Beth.

> Gray: Don't contact me anymore it's causing problems with my woman.

> Beth: I'm so sorry, Gray. I knew it was an issue. Thank you for everything.

Shit!

I was going to kill her.

"Kayla!" My voice boomed through the house, and I knew she heard me, but she was hiding like the guilty little snake she was. Instead of texting back I called Beth who was sniffling on the other end when she picked up.

"I'm so sorry, Gray. I didn't mean to..."

"Beth, stop. I didn't send you that message this morning. Hell, I probably never would have known about it had my phone not started ringing while Kayla was fuckin' with it."

"Wh-what?"

"Yeah, seems Kayla and I are going to have a come to Jesus talk a lot sooner than I thought," I sighed. "I tried hanging in here to make sure she had someone helping her out since she literally has no one. I can't be that someone any longer though. There's a reason she has no one, and you just saw a little bit of that."

"Oh my God, who does that kind of thing? I'm sorry you're caught up with someone like that, Gray, but don't let your hero complex keep you in a situation you don't want to be in any longer. Life is too short." She would know that better than anyone. Life was far too short to spend it not being happy every minute you could, because sometimes you needed those happy moments to fill the void when everything went wrong.

"Yeah, I'm seeing that for what it is now, trust me. I just wanted to make sure you were okay, and that you knew the reality of that text. Do not ever hesitate to call me if you need anything, and if you can't get a hold of me you use the numbers Ghost gave you. The guys will see to whatever you need."

"I don't know how to begin to thank you, Gray. My life changed that night in ways that I never would have understood before, but if you hadn't been the one... If you hadn't cared... I don't know where Abby and I would be right now."

"Right place, right time, sweetheart. Kiss Abby for me. I have to go get ready for some club business, but I'll give you a call and check in later."

"Thanks again, Gray, and stay safe when you're out there riding."

"Sure thing," I told her before hanging up, and getting my butt in gear. I didn't bother hunting down Kayla because that's what she wanted when she hid away. I was done playing her games. I had just finished getting ready and snagged a go cup with coffee when Kayla finally emerged from wherever she'd been hiding out.

"Weren't you going to come say goodbye?" she asked in her sugary sweet voice as if she hadn't done something to make me angry.

"Nope," I answered as I stirred a little bit of cream into my coffee.

"Where are you going? You aren't supposed to go to the clubhouse until this evening."

"Shit changed; I've got a run to make."

"When will you be back?" The bitchy Kayla called out instead of the sweet one.

"I don't fuckin' know, Kayla," I spat out, exasperated with her personality flips. "When I do get back, we're sitting down and having a fuckin' heart-to-heart kind of conversation though. That shit you pulled with my phone – not cool. I can't fuckin' believe you'd stoop to that level of deceit, but you crossed a major fuckin' line with me."

Her face pinched up while her eyes narrowed on me. "It's always about her! What about me?"

"What about you? What the fuck about you, Kayla? That woman lost her husband and two of her children. I'm just trying to help her out, because that shit is rough on a person, and she doesn't have any other family."

"I don't have any other family either," Kayla spat out.

"You do. You just ruined those relationships with your antics. The difference between Beth and you is that her life was taken from her; all of it out of her control. You threw yours away on stupid, spoiled, rich girl decisions that got you into trouble. You did it to yourself."

"Why are you here then?" she shouted at me.

"I ask myself that on a daily basis these days, because you are not the person that I thought you were, and I'm seeing there's really not a big hope in hell that you'll ever be more than this." I waved a hand in her direction indicating the whole miserable package that she was.

"There's nothing worse than a chick who would start

drama with a woman who lost most of her family, because you're jealous that all the attention isn't on you. I don't know who the fuck you are, but you are not someone I want to give my time to these days."

"I'm sorry, Gray!" The sweet Kayla was back and whining. "I let it get the best of me, and I was jealous, because I thought you would end up leaving me for her."

I laughed. "She just lost her husband and children, Kayla. There's nothing romantic about that situation. If you had put forth more of an effort, you could have been helping her too and been right there beside me every time I went to check on them. I asked you to come along, remember? You did it at first when she was in the hospital, but then it was too much to ask of you."

"I didn't think…" she started, but I cut her off.

"You never do! That's the problem. We'll talk about all this later, because right now I have somewhere else to be."

With that, I headed for the clubhouse to meet up with Smoke, and whoever else was heading out on what would be my first official run with the club.

THREE HOURS LATER, I found myself driving the box van that claimed to be hauling auto parts, but I was pretty sure was stuffed full of guns and ammo. I didn't really give a rat's ass about laws and breaking or abiding by them, so it never occurred to me ask what the club was into aside from the legit businesses they had in Cedar Falls like the pawn shop and the bar down the street from the club-house. There was also a diner owned by one of the brothers and his old lady, though I was murky on whether it was a personal venture or part of the club's legit businesses too.

Since the other prospect, Mouth, hadn't shown for duty and Hold 'Em was busy on a separate run I was sitting in the van alone on this trip instead of having a partner with me as the guys had originally planned. Smoke, Heavy, Wren, and Ghost were on the run too, but the guys were riding in pairs with two leading the way and two trailing behind. We were just passing close to the state line when the blue lights and siren lit up the road. "Fuck!"

"We're gonna haul ass, catch his attention, and hope he follows us instead of you," Smoke called over the open line we'd had for communication.

"Do what you do, I have it handled here."

They did their thing. All four bikes took off like the hounds of hell were nipping at their heels. Taking off in such a manner made them look guilty, obviously, because the cop flew past me in hot pursuit. The problem with that scenario was that there had been two pickup trucks behind the police cruiser and two Harleys behind them. As soon as the cruiser and my boys were out of sight everything started going down.

The blue Ford F-350 took off, appeared at first to be following the cop into the pursuit, but all too quickly he swerved right in front of me, clipping my bumper, and causing me to swerve a bit before I got control again.

"Son of a..."

"What's going on?" I heard Smoke call out since he hadn't been able to disconnect with me yet.

"Truck just clipped the front bumper nearly sent me off the... Holy fuck!" I slammed on breaks as the truck in front of me had just done, and while I tried to pull around him at the same time, I was unable to because the second truck had already pulled around to flank me in the oncoming traffic lane.

"I'm being boxed in by two pickup trucks and," I glanced in my rearview to see the bikes more clearly. "Looks like two Harleys with riders wearing kuttes that do not belong to Aces High."

"Shit!" Smoke bellowed from his end. "They used the cops to separate us from the load."

Smoke started barking orders that were apparently for the other guys on the bikes. I was busy pulling the van over and throwing it in park as quickly and safely as I could, because they definitely had me pinned in good. I wasn't going down as a corpse out here though. I grabbed the Glock I had stuffed in my waistband and took aim on the passenger in the truck that had flanked me. I popped a round off, hitting him, though not in the head so he might live through this one.

Then shots were returned at the van. "Don't hit the fuckin' merchandise," someone shouted.

"The asshole is shooting at us. He already clipped ShortStack."

My seat belt was released, and I was crawling toward the passenger side door when a voice called out from the driver's side window that I had kept down for the fresh air. "Not so fast, asshole!" I didn't think, just reacted, took aim, and shot the motherfucker before he could shoot me. I was pretty sure that one was going to be Dead on Arrival when the law and emergency crews finally got on scene, because he took a bullet right between the eyes.

"Fuck, fuck, fuck! Marshall's down!" Someone yelled, and if I was counting right that meant there were two down and three or four more to go depending on how many were in the truck taking point. The distant rumble of motorcycle engines spurred everyone into action. I wasn't sure if they would be friendlies or backup for the assholes attacking, so I got busy.

I took aim again, out the passenger side window, and managed to hit one of the guys creeping up the side of the van in the leg. He screamed and went down grabbing at his wound about the same time the back door to the van was wrenched open. I spun and fired, hitting the man who barreled into the van like an idiot. That was four of a possible six that had been hit now. As I went to lean back behind the passenger seat again, I felt a searing heat in my left bicep and spun in time to take out the man who had just shot me. Luckily for me, his aim was shit, and I was just grazed.

Unlucky for him, my aim was superb, and his ass was dead. The truck in front of the van suddenly pulled out and spun around in the direction it had originally come from as the roaring engines of my future club brothers got progressively louder as they were finally coming into view up ahead.

There were only three. Heavy, having been the odd man out, was chosen to drag the cop further away from the action going down. As the others rode up, one of the wounded men began shooting, so I turned and shot him once more. That meant he had a shoulder wound to tend to along with the bullet I'd already put in his thigh.

"Well, Goddamn, Gray, you didn't leave shit for us to do," Wren called out before laughing the tension away.

Smoke was up at the side of the van in no time assessing my state and seeing if I needed medical assistance. "I'm good," I told him. "Just winged me, dude."

"There were six total. One of them got away in that truck as you were rolling up. It was obvious what they were here for though." I tipped my head toward the fabricated panels that hid everything I'd been hauling.

Ghost and Wren had been busy rounding up the wounded men and tying them up on the side of the road while I updated Smoke.

"Fuck man, the Army taught you right," Wren commented as he took note of the wounded and the two that were not coming back from what I'd done to them.

"Call it in and get someone out here to help clean this shit up," Ghost bellowed. "We can use their truck to haul the bikes back soon as we get this shit settled, but we need to be quick about it. No telling how long Heavy can hold off the cops before he ends up thrown in fuckin' jail for his efforts." Ghost leaned in the van and looked at me then, also assessing where I was with everything. "Good job, son. We'll see to your wound in just a bit."

"No need," I called back to him, already reaching for the first aid kit I brought with me. I pulled out some gauze, dripped some peroxide down the cut that was deep enough it would need stitching, and then I plopped the gauze over top and wrapped it tight. It would do for now.

"Well shit," Ghost muttered. "Never had one of our guys get shot and field dress the wound on his own before. That's a new one." He shook his head back and forth as he moved closer to the assholes tied up on the side of the road. "Let's see which one of you pricks will be spending time in our special room back at the clubhouse." He then completely fucked with their head by pulling out "Eeny, meeny, miny, moe" at which point Wren burst out laughing again.

"That's some fucked up shit, Ghost." The man chuckled and kept going until he got to the part of "You are not it." Except when he got there it was a corpse, he'd landed on, so he added in, "Because you're already dead, fucker!"

"Jesus!" That was from Smoke as he shook his head at our club president's antics.

"Seriously, pick two, get them loaded up in the van for now. We need to get away from this shit show as quick as possible. Crusher and Court are waiting for us just over the line."

Smoke grabbed two of the assholes, tossed them in the back of the van, and left one of them there on the side of the road with his dead buddies. "This should give you something to think about, maybe consider a life change, Hound." Smoke's cool voice rolled through the air like a shot. "Let your brethren know we have their boys, they keep fuckin' around with our runs and we'll see that those boys do not enjoy their stay. Let Tonka know we'll be in touch."

With that, the better of the two bikes plus Smoke's ride, were loaded up in the truck. We couldn't fit the third, because Smoke's bike was a monster taking up most of the room all by itself. Smoke got behind the wheel, Ghost and

Wren hopped back on their bikes, and we all took off for the rendezvous point with Crusher and Court.

Both men were Aces High members from the Tallahassee Chapter. They would be taking over the shipment once we got to them and heading south with it. Where the shipment would end up was anyone's guess, and not my business to know as a prospect so I didn't bother to ask any questions.

We didn't really have time for questions anyway since we were trying to avoid the police and had to take an alternate route back to the clubhouse after dropping off the box van to the guys from Tallahassee. Their van had mechanical problems on the way, so I ended up relinquishing ours and hopping in the truck we'd procured from the Hell Hounds MC members that had attacked us. Smoke continued to drive, and I started getting nervous when he kept glancing at me.

"Dude? What's up?"

He shook his head in disbelief and then let me in on his thoughts. "You, surfer man. You're chill as ice over there like you didn't get shot today and didn't kill a couple guys and leave a few more injured all by your lonesome until we could get back to you."

"Am I supposed to be freaking the fuck out?" I asked honestly, not knowing what he expected.

"Nah, man. I just don't think any of our other prospects would be so cool under pressure. I'd place money that had it been Mouth in your spot he would have been dead before he even popped one shot off, yet here you sit like nothing happened, not freaking the fuck out, and not asking questions about why you were shot at."

I laughed then. "Something about me you might not know since I talk surfer slow and all, but I totally have a brain, dude." I said this with an affected surfer drawl before chuckling. "I'll tell you what I know. The shipment we just dropped was guns and ammo. I know this because the smell of fuckin' lubricating oil was a bit strong in the van when I got in, and it has a different smell to what you would get from car parts.

"Seeing as those dudes were wearing patches with a different logo and club name on them, and they were all about shooting first and taking names later, I was able to put together for myself that they were a rival club. This was later confirmed when you and Ghost spoke to the men. So, I'm pretty much up to speed on what's going down and don't need to ask unnecessary questions."

"It doesn't bother you that we're runnin' guns?"

I simply shrugged. "Would it bother me had the cop followed me, there weren't any rivals to take him out, and I got popped for hauling 'em? I'd probably be a bit miffed, because I just don't look good in day-glow orange, man. Plus, jumpsuits tend to ride up on the balls, and that's just not cool."

Smoke burst out laughing so hard I thought he'd have to pull the fuck over, but he got his shit together quick enough and just shook his head at me once more. "Fuckin' Christ. It's like someone put you in the perfect biker-man mold and spit you out."

"I do what I can," I offered smugly and buffed my nails on the leather of my kutte as Smoke continued to chuckle.

"Fuckin' hell! Ghost needs to give me an award for recruiting your ass."

I glanced down at my arm as he said that and notice the blood had oozed through the gauze and bandaging in a major way. "I'm gonna need some stitches when we get back. You know how, or have someone there that can handle it without making me look like fuckin' Frankenstein's monster?"

Smoke grinned. "The fact that you know the difference between Frankenstein and the monster means you're too fuckin' smart for this shit, but whatever. Yeah, I can pop a couple stitches in you. Won't be my first time sewing a brother back together either, so you can keep looking sunshine and surf ready, dude."

The 'dude' part was said with a mock, slowness that I just laughed off. Then I huffed out a sigh as we pulled into the compound, because it was damn good to be back home. Home meant I could do something about the ache in my arm, finally. I might be cool under pressure, but getting shot still stung like a son of a bitch.

7. DUPLICITOUS

It became apparent, almost immediately, that I would not be doing something about the ache in my arm just yet, because once we moved through the doors of the clubhouse, I had a clear view of the pool tables and the familiar head of hair that was there, bobbing back and forth on a club brother I'd never seen before. I didn't even think before moving across the room. The shit with Beth may have been the last straw, but I wasn't about to be disrespected in a place I had just gotten shot up to be a part of.

"You have got to be fucking kidding me," came out of my mouth as I charged forward.

"Shit!" I heard Smoke yell from somewhere behind me, as he had delayed coming in with me in order to get his bike off the truck so another brother could go ditch the truck. Damn thing was stolen property and we didn't need it hanging around as evidence to what went down.

As soon as I was within swinging distance, I clocked the motherfucker, who had been receiving a blowjob from my girlfriend, right in his downturned nose. He never saw it coming because he had been too busy watching her work him over.

"Gray!" I heard my name hissed out in surprise from Kayla and the minute she caught my wild-eyed look she got off her knees and backed up.

"He didn't know, man!" Smoke was there getting between the asshole with his cock still hanging out and me.

"The fuck?" The bleeding man roared. "You let a fuckin' prospect hit a brother and not a fuckin' one of you does shit about it?"

"Fuck you, asshole!" I yelled at him and went in for another hit before I was lifted bodily off my feet and set back down further away from the man. Truth be told, I only went after him because I couldn't hit who I really wanted to. Fucking Kayla. I didn't want her anymore, but this shit was the height of disrespect. She was blowing a brother in my own home, so to speak. Sure, I was nothing more than a prospect, but still. This was the place I planned to lay down my roots and she was here sullying that shit.

Ghost appeared out of thin air then and got in my face. "Traveler is nomad, and didn't know who she was," he told me calmly while keeping both of his hands firmly planted on my shoulders.

"Get him the fuck out of here, he just fucked up his prospect period," the guy Ghost called Traveler yelled.

"You're just pissed he got the drop on you in the middle of getting your cock sucked," one of the guys howled out in peals of laughter.

Smoke stepped in when it looked like Traveler was ready

to throw down with someone else. "Stop. We're not saying shit to him, because any one of us would have done the same fuckin' thing if we walked in the club and saw our old lady suckin' another brother's cock. You feel me?"

"What? Old lady?" Traveler turned toward the duplicitous bitch in question. "You have an old man involved in this club?" Now, it looked like there was another man wanting to put his hands on her, and not in the way she wanted.

Kayla simply shrugged, still managing to pull off her wide, doe-eyed look of surprise like she didn't realize she'd been sucking cock in the clubhouse. "I can't really be his old lady since he's not a member. So, not really," she attempted to cover for herself.

"The fact we've been together for two and a half years means you shouldn't have been suckin' another man's dick. The fact I'm prospecting for this club means it sure as fuck shouldn't have happened here."

"You were going to leave me tonight anyway; I just know it. You left mad, because of what I did to Beth," she started to say and stopped the minute she heard several people suck in a breath. That was when she realized she was really in trouble with the club.

"What the fuck did she do to Beth?" Smoke called out through clenched teeth.

"That's for later, I already handled it." I told the guys before turning back to Kayla. "I don't even know who the fuck you are anymore."

"I didn't want to wait to be accepted as a real old lady," she spat back, going back to her argument about me not being a real brother and just a prospect, a position I was bound to hold for at least a year according to tales I'd heard from the other guys about how long it took them to get patched in.

"You sure as fuck will never be accepted as anything but club pussy, now," Ghost informed her. "And after this, no member will touch you, so you won't even be that."

Ghost turned to me then, clapped his hand back on my shoulder, and sighed. "It's good to know this now, son. You patch in on Friday officially so that gives us time to get your kutte ready, and the party all set. You survived trial by fire for us tonight, so you deserve it. Let that be a consolation, considering what you came home to after being shot."

"Wait, you're a full member now?" Regret laced Kayla's features, but what wasn't there was concern for the fact that I had been shot to earn my place in the brotherhood this soon.

"You got what you wanted just in time to suck it all away for yourself. Now, I need to go clear my shit from the house."

"No! Wait! I'm sorry, Gray. I wasn't thinking."

"You weren't thinking when you pulled that stunt with Beth this morning. You weren't thinking when you figured it was okay to suck another brother's cock at the clubhouse in plain sight. Did you think at all today?" I held a hand up to stave off her answer. "Don't bother because you know who has been thinking? Me. The things I've been thinking for a while now are that I'm done with your shit. I'm done with you being a toxic nothingness that wastes my resources, and I'm fuckin' over dealing with the fallout of your dramas on the regular. So, good luck with your house, and your life after, but none of it will include me, because I've been thinking about a lot and I'm just plain fucking done." I turned my back on her then and glanced over at Smoke.

"I've got you covered, brother. You come stay at my place, and as soon as we get your arm tended, we'll grab one of the vans and head over to get your shit."

"You're not welcome back in my house if you do this, so good luck getting your shit. I'll call the cops and tell them I don't know who you are. I'll tell them it's all mine, and you're stealing from me. They'll lock you up for doing it."

"Lock this bitch up," Ghost called out.

"Gladly," Wren stated as he took hold of Kayla and dragged her out of the main area.

"Wh-what are you doing? Get your hands off me! This is kidnapping! I'll call my dad and have every fucking cop and federal agent in this place in minutes."

I laughed. "Your dad isn't lifting a finger to help you anymore, because you screwed over one of his best friends, remember? Besides, I've kept him abreast of the fact that you haven't changed a fuckin' bit."

"You what?" she spat the question back at me.

"He called for a while to check on you at your mother's behest. I told him how you were doing. I never lied. He told me if it ever got too bad to let him know and he'd come out to have you committed and put in a facility for treatment. He never did spill your secrets or why he wanted to know though, so at least you should be thankful he still respected your privacy enough not to let on about what went down so you could maybe have a fresh start."

This was all true and should have been a huge red flag, but I honestly thought it was just a play due to his anger over what his daughter had done. Obviously, he thought she had to be off her rocker a bit to fuck over his friend the way she had. After seeing the way that she attempted to manipulate the situation with Beth and then tonight, I was leaning more towards agreeing with him. It wasn't just that she had grown up spoiled. Something was seriously wrong with her.

"We'll hold her a couple hours while you get your shit together. Let us know when you get it all, and we'll make sure she gets home in one piece."

"You can't do this!" Kayla was screaming from down the hall again. Then I couldn't hear her, and I assumed Wren had taken her down to the basement where there were three special soundproof rooms. We had two occupied with the Hell Hounds who had attacked me earlier, but there was a third room downstairs sitting empty and waiting. Served her right.

"You're welcome to stay as long as you like, and don't worry about being in my way. I'm spend most of my time over at Poppy's these days. She has Bubba, and he needs the yard, which is something I don't have here. I can't have pets in this place anyway. So, you'll mostly be on your own." Smoke laid it out for me as he showed me around his three-bedroom apartment.

"Dude, why are you paying for a three-bedroom place for just you?"

"I had roommates before, but they were both fuckwads.

When they left, I just decided to keep the place on my own since I'm on the top floor, and in a corner unit It cuts down on the noise from neighbors on the days when I was off shift and need sleep at odd hours."

"I hear you there. Our last place in San Diego we had this big guy above us, sounded like a herd of cattle running through the apartment when he moved around up there. This dude was like six feet, seven inches of solid, thick muscle and didn't know a thing about walking gently."

Smoke laughed. "Yeah, I've had all kinds. The chick that lived next door in my last place was a screamer, and our bedroom walls adjoined. My ex-girlfriend, Julie and I used to either try to outdo her moans sometimes or find the best fuckin' noise canceling earplugs and headphones money could buy. It was insane."

He grabbed two beers out of the fridge and handed one to me. "Come to think of it, I think she was a working girl or something, because it was all the fuckin' time, and never the same man walking out of her door in the morning."

"Damn, dude, that's tough. Let me know what my share of the rent and bills will be. You know I have no problem paying it, and I'm not looking for a handout."

"It's all good man, we'll talk about that shit tomorrow. Let's tend to your bandage there and add a little more ointment to that wound before you turn in for the night."

"Sure thing, sweet cheeks," I teased. "You take such good care of me snook'ems."

"Fuck! I knew I'd regret setting your ass up with a room."

I blew him a kiss as he retrieved the first aid kit. "I'll see about snagging some antibiotics from the hospital tomorrow, just in case."

"Yeah, be sure you don't pop any of my beautiful stitching on the job too while you're at it. You know you shouldn't be lifting anything heavy, but I'm sure that warning won't stop you."

I just shrugged. "I'll be cautious."

Smoke took a hard look at me then. "I know that things haven't been good between you guys lately, but it had to suck walkin' in on that shit tonight, especially after the day you had."

I just shook my head. "Nah dude, that's the thing. I know I was months past being done with her shit, because it didn't bother me outside of the fact that she made me look bad at the clubhouse. I had planned to talk to you tonight about seeing if I could rent a room for a bit until I could find a place anyway, because I was already finished with her. I hadn't planned on another night in that house." I told him what she had done about Beth when we were packing my things up earlier and had to stop him from going back to the clubhouse to unleash on her.

"Still can't believe she didn't think you'd find out about the stunt she was trying to pull with Beth."

"If you hadn't called, I'm sure she would have covered her tracks and Beth would have been too polite to mention it. So, she was probably right in thinking that I wouldn't have known."

"Well, fuck, sorry you got shot today then, but not sorry I called at the right time."

I laughed. "Yeah, thanks for that. Your call got my ass shot, dude!"

"It also got you patched in as a full brother in just a few months rather than waiting the typical twelve to eighteen."

"True."

"Plus, they only winged you, so quit your bitchin' already, pansy-ass." Smoke's phone pinged with an incoming message. He glanced down at it and smiled. "Looks like your ex is going to manage to hold her tongue despite the fit she threw earlier."

"Yeah? How'd they manage that miracle?"

"Did we ever tell you that we have cameras in the clubhouse? Everything gets wiped at the end of the night if there's nothing useful on the feed, but we've determined after countless incidents that it's best not to inform the prospects before they're patched, you feel?"

"I get that. So, you caught her on camera, huh?"

Smoke nodded. "The guys let her know that no one would believe shit she had to say when we showed that she was there willingly to cheat on you with another brother, and that she was just acting out and making shit up since she was pissed that she got caught and lost access to your bank account as a result."

I laughed then. "Good, it's about time she found out the world doesn't revolve around her shit."

"Yeah, and just so you are aware, she was given the edict by Ghost that she is persona non grata at the clubhouse, near the brothers, or properties and businesses the club is involved with. The guys all got the message that she's banished too."

I breathed a sigh of relief. "I'm fuckin' stoked to hear that shit, dude! That's really fuckin' good, because it gives me a chance to actually start with a clean slate without her showing up and bringing her drama around," I explained, probably needlessly, because I'm pretty sure he understood. Then Smoke took off not long after that to head to Poppy's house while I got settled into my new living situation.

8. THE PATCH

Friday was the big day, and despite how fucking ecstatic I was to be living it, there were certain people who weren't exactly happy that I was jumping them in line to the throne, so to speak. The other prospects, even when they were being courteous, were giving me side-long glances that ran the gamut from mildly curious – Hold 'Em - to downright distrustful – Mouth.

The latter should have been on the run that changed things for me but wasn't because he'd bailed for personal shit. I understood his anger and Hold 'Em's curiosity, to a point. They wanted to know why they'd all been prospecting longer than me, and yet I was the one being patched over. I supposed Ghost hadn't spread the news of what happened on our run far and wide.

The second thing that struck me – after the funny looks I garnered from the prospects – was that without Kayla tagging along I wasn't nearly as edgy as I normally was. Feeling the loss of the weight I once carried on my shoulders,

I knew I did the right thing in leaving her, but the wrong thing in staying with her as long as I had. I hadn't realized just how toxic she had become to me. My stress levels were greatly reduced now that I was done with her, and I wasn't waiting for the other shoe to drop all the time. My life was suddenly looking all kinds of sunshiny and bright as fuck.

I also noticed the respect levels from the brothers toward myself increased. Whether that was because I got shy of Kayla or because I was becoming one of them officially, I wasn't certain. Hell, it could have been a little bit of both. Either way I wasn't looking that gift horse in the mouth.

Nope, I was soaking it all in and waiting for the big moment when I officially became a part of the Aces High MC. I hadn't been too keen on moving from Cali to West Virginia when Kayla first mentioned it, but now that I was here, I felt like I was finally home and part of that feeling had to do with the MC.

"You noticed the difference, huh?" Smoke's voice came from just over my shoulder as I took everything in.

"It's a little insane, yeah."

He slapped a hand down on my shoulder. "Everyone here respects the shit out of you, Gray. I'm sure they've all wondered why you were with Crazy Kayla, and it wasn't any of their fuckin' business. I admire you for sticking it out and trying the way you did. Sometimes, people give up too soon and miss out. Other times, it's a fuckin' wash, but how are you going to know unless you give it your all in an honest way?"

I turned to see the sincerity on his face. He grinned in return. "I was with the wrong woman for five fuckin' years, man. Just be glad you got shy of this one sooner than that. Not for nothing but sticking it out as long as you did led you here to us, and that's what I would focus on."

"That is exactly why I'm not considering it a lost couple years," I admitted as I shook my head. "She wasn't all bad in the beginning, but she's definitely not good enough for the headaches I endured."

"Amen, brother." He tapped his shoulder to mine then and tipped his head in the direction of the bar instantly causing my breath to catch in my lungs. They were here.

"You guys invited them?"

"Of course, we did. Beth wouldn't have missed this for the world. We did encourage them to leave once you get your kutte though since shit tends to get crazy."

"What if I don't want her to leave?" The question left my lips in a reverent tone that Smoke didn't miss.

He smirked and then turned so the women who were now watching us couldn't see his mouth moving as he spoke. "I'm going to assume you don't mean Beth, but I will warn you they showed together, so they're a package deal tonight." He turned his head enough to glance over at the women. "She's skittish though, so I'd take your time with that one or risk scaring her off."

"Yeah, I noticed." My admission made me realize I still hadn't managed to get her story. I knew she had a kid with her same last name, and I hadn't yet seen evidence of a man in her life. There was no ring on her finger, I had checked. Not that it meant much. Lots of people back home in Cali didn't bother with the ring, or if they did it was only as some sick status symbol indicating the amount of money spent, not what the ring was supposed to symbolize.

I asked Beth once and she just told me she wasn't going to gossip about her best friend. In the nicest way possible – entirely Beth's style – she told me to man up and ask her myself, but only after Kayla was out of the picture. I had the utmost respect for Beth and had promised her I would do just that. It looked like tonight might finally be the night when I got to hold true to that promise.

"All right, assholes, listen up!" I turned my attention to Ghost who was standing on the raised portion of the main room in the clubhouse, so he was looking down on everyone gathered around. "As most of you all know, tonight we're all here to pay homage to our newest brother. He was our newest prospect, and yet he managed to win everyone's respect without even trying. He was just being himself. Right, dude?" he asked, drawing out the last word in perfect So-Cal fashion. I tossed up a Shaka sign with my pinky and thumb out while the rest of my fingers closed to my palm. I waved it at him in good surfer-boy fashion which resulted in a room full of chuckles before he waved his hands at the crowd to get them to quiet down again.

"Thing is, he really was just being himself. Then, the fucker had to go and bleed for the club. He proved himself not only capable and loyal, but invaluable in one of the most stressful situations a man can ever be tested in. For that, above all, he earned his kutte earlier than most." The man turned and pointed out each prospect in the room. "The rest of you are doing great. Don't think we aren't noticing hard work when it gets put in. This is a special circumstance, due to trial by fire, and I know each of you knows exactly what that means." The three prospects each nodded their head. "Except Mouth, who couldn't be bothered to show up the day Gray earned his kutte. Let that be a lesson to you. Gray's not prospecting for us any longer because he showed up and handled his shit. Think on that."

Without hesitation, Ghost waggled the index fingers on both of his hands at someone, two of them actually, and to my surprise Gillian and Beth were escorted up to his makeshift stage. "These ladies have been blessed with getting to know our Surfer-Medic and asked that they be able to participate in tonight's festivities even though it's a bit unorthodox for a non-member to do so. I felt that Surfer would be amenable to the situation though."

Fucking Ghost and his big words. Half the men here probably didn't understand what he was saying. I did not miss the fact that he continued to call me some variation of surfer though. I sighed inwardly knowing what road name was headed my way.

"Daniel Gray Grayson come on up here!" Ghost's bellowing voice echoed through the unusually quiet space making it feel far more cavernous than all the hot bodies packed into it made it seem. I moved quickly to the spot where Ghost stood with Gillian and Beth who both beamed beautiful smiles my way. When I stopped just in front of them Ghost grinned down at me. "Do you accept your position as full member, in good standing, with the Aces High Motorcycle Club?" I nodded my head as the words of acknowledgment left my mouth.

"I do," I stated coolly, even though I felt like I was getting married instead of joining an MC.

"He does," Ghost intoned and then laughed with half the damn club members. Yeah, wrong choice of words. "Ladies," Ghost called out. "Let's show him that gorgeous kutte." As soon as the words were out of his mouth the women moved and maneuvered my hands into the arm holes on the leather vest and then slid it up my shoulders.

I glanced down to see that I hadn't been wrong, even as I groaned at the thought of that becoming my name from now until my final days.

"Welcome to Aces High, Surfer!" Ghost proclaimed as he watched me drag my fingers across the embroidered patch with my name on it. Both women hugged me quickly and then stood off to the side while each brother took their turn coming up to congratulate me with a punch to the chest, right over my new name. By the end of the procession that shit hurt like a mother fucker, not that you'd ever hear me complain about it out loud. They'd literally just pounded my new name into my flesh so it would never be forgotten.

9. CELEBRATING

ONCE EVERYONE HAD THEIR FILL, I REALIZED THAT I COULDN'T FIND Beth in the crowd. "Where's Beth?" I finally asked Smoke when I found him.

"She needed to get home. Hold' 'Em took her so you wouldn't have to be worried." He looked like he was waiting on me to say something, his grin growing wider the longer it took me. "Really not gonna ask?"

I shrugged my shoulders, sipped from the bottle of beer in my hand and casually glanced around the clubhouse once more. Smoke laughed before clapping me on the back. "Poppy took Gillian to show her where the restroom was. Apparently, there's a clean one the ladies don't mind using and then there's the rest of the dirty bastard bathrooms they try not to mess around in.

"Who?" I asked, playing dumb.

"Uh huh, you keep playing that game, Surfer, we'll see how far you get with it."

I grinned over the top of my bottle before taking another

sip. He knew exactly who I'd been looking for. "She gonna be okay with Poppy, you know, by themselves? Lots of out-of-town men here tonight."

"They'll be just fine," Smoke stated evenly. "I have a prospect trailing them in case anyone shows too much interest." I didn't think any of the Aces High men would ever do anything without a woman's permission, but I also didn't know them all and I knew bad apples could fall just about anywhere.

"That makes me feel better," I admitted. Then my nose scrunched up when I thought about the fact that the only prospect I really trusted was gone with Beth.

Smoke laughed, guessing where my train of thought went. "Don't worry, I put D on it. I knew better then to ask Mouth." I nodded my appreciation. Thank fuck. "Now, tell me, are you gonna actually do something about your attraction to her?"

"Now that I'm single and not trying to figure out where to stow my baggage?" I questioned with a smirk. "Yeah, that was the plan."

"Well, get your A-game together then because here she comes." He tipped his head in the direction of the back hall just where the pool table was set up in the corner. She laughed at something Poppy was saying to her and it didn't take a genius to see that the two women were drawing interest from the crowd of men around them. As soon as one attempted to swoop in, the prospect was right on top of it, and the women didn't even seem to notice the cock-blocking he was doing.

"That kid is smooth," I noted. Smoke laughed.

"He's gunning to be the next prospect through sheer dint of will. Brass balls too, being willing to go up against brothers like that."

"Hey," Gillian's sweet voice called out over the music that pumped through the place just a touch too loudly. I heard her anyway as I watched the way her lips formed that one word.

"Come on," I grabbed onto her arm and guided her outside to the multilevel decks the club had out back.

"Wow, this is amazing."

"Yeah, they know how to maximize the space for enter-taining," I agreed as we shuffled off to a far corner to take a seat on a bench. I turned my back to the action that was happening in the hot tub on another deck and just smiled at the woman before me. "You stayed," I commented.

She nodded her head at the same time she let her hair cascade down to cover the blush that built on her cheeks. "I stayed." I tipped her chin up so that she had to look at me then. "Part of me feels guilty for it," she admitted.

"Why is that?"

"You were with someone else when I first started falling for you." I was floored by her admission.

"Can't tell you how much I wish that I'd gotten shy of her before I met you. Knew she was toxic. Hell, I'd been talking to Smoke about what I was going to do and how I just didn't want to leave her high and dry since I knew she didn't have anyone else."

"Stop," she got out as she put her hand up to my mouth. "I know all that too. I'm not blind. If I'm being honest, it was part of what I found so attractive about you. Most men wouldn't hesitate to bail if they weren't feeling it anymore, never mind the consequences for that other person they once cared about. You stuck it out until she made it impossible for you to do that. I admired you for it even while I wanted to throttle her for being so damn stupid."

I kissed her fingertips that were still lying gently against my lips and then I pulled them down, so our hands were entwined sitting on my lap. "Who has Kade tonight?"

"Oh, Kade's grandma took him and Abby so we could come tonight, but Beth is picking them up and taking them back to her place for the night. That's why she left early. I don't like leaving Kade overnight with his grandma.

"Why is that?"

"His dad isn't in his life, but I know he shows up there sometimes. She mentioned he only comes late at night though when he thinks she won't notice."

"That's kind of weird."

"I think so too, and it's also the reason I don't let my son stay the night there."

"Is your ex a problem? Are you afraid he'll hurt you or Kade?"

"Nothing like that. He's just..." she sighed. "We weren't important enough to him to stick around for. He signed over his rights to Kade as soon it was obvious the baby was his." She rolled her eyes then. "It was always obvious to me since he was the only man I'd ever been with, but when a man wants out of his responsibilities, he'll say and believe anything." She waved away her own comment.

"Anyway, once Kade was born and I told him we'd done our part of the DNA test, he just asked to sign papers relinquishing custody. The woman he had been cheating on me with required a ring on her finger and for him not to have a baby with anyone else."

"Are you kidding me? And he still married her knowing he had a kid on the way?"

I nodded my head. "Yeah, so since she was determined that she wouldn't be with him if our baby was his, he made damn sure to legally make it so I couldn't come after him for child support or any other obligations. He had the papers ready for me to sign before I could even take Kade out of the hospital."

"What a fucking dirtbag!"

"Yeah, I'm kind of glad he did it though. When we first got together, we were in high school. It didn't take long before he started changing though. Once he could drive and ride his motorcycle things started becoming strained. He was gone a lot but would never tell me where he was headed or where he'd been. Around the time I found out I was pregnant I started realizing he was cheating too. I don't think that's where he was gone to all that time though. He fell in with some pretty unsavory people. I don't want my son around that."

"You said motorcycles. Is he in a club?" she shrugged her shoulders.

"I honestly don't know. I always assumed maybe he was, but no one has ever confirmed it and I've never seen him wearing anything like this," she explained as her fingers traced over the name on my kutte. She chuckled then added my new name, and coming from her sweet lips, it didn't sound so bad. "Surfer."

"Yeah, these dudes are dicks for that," I mentioned as I laughed with her.

"Well," Gillian hedged as she sat back and took in my appearance. "You do have the look with your sun-bleached curls and then there's the fact that you still call everyone dude. Who does that?"

"I do that," I insisted as I dove in tickling her. "The people who ask that question suffer the consequences too."

Her giggles twisted my insides in a way I'd never felt before. I could almost die a happy man if that was the last sound that I heard on this earth. I slowed my movements as she doubled over to protect her middle which put her almost in my lap. My fingers traced slowly up her sides, then across her shoulders until I could pull her in closer to me. Her head tipped back, and her bright green eyes glimmered in the faint firelight from the pit someone had thoughtfully started a fire in.

"Gillian," I whispered before taking her mouth with mine.

There it was. Kissing Gillian showed me that I wasn't wrong about missing something with Kayla all that time. There was the rush you felt when you were with someone because everything was new and exciting, but then there was this entirely different, all-consuming feeling. It was an intense zing of chemistry. Judging by her response when I pulled away, I wasn't the only one to feel it.

"Whoa," she hummed out as our lips separated. Worry laced her eyes then. "What about Kayla? Are you sure?"

"I'm sure as I'll ever be that she is my past. I meant what I said. She's toxic. I should have known early on. Her father came to visit me after we'd been dating a couple months. I guess he had someone keeping tabs on her and noticed that she was getting her shit together. He told me I had to be the reason for her turn around, but that if she ever started back-sliding to let him know and he'd handle whatever trouble she caused."

"That's strange," Gillian commented.

"It was, but she'd already told me that her parents disowned her because they didn't approve of what she wanted to do with her life. She was in school to be a phle-botomist. I thought maybe because they were so rich, they saw that as beneath them. Where I'm from its not unheard of for some of those rich kids to be treated that way for wanting a normal life, you know?" she acknowledged that with a tip of her head, so I continued.

"Anyway, I guess he kept on keeping tabs, and my buddy showed up not long after that wanting me to head up the coast with him to Oregon. He was patching into the club he'd been a part of when he was a kid, finally, and he wanted to bring me along for the ride."

"Another MC?"

"Yeah, the StoneRidge Raiders. They're a smaller club with less charters around, but they're still decent sized. They wore the one-percenters patch though, so it gave me pause."

"One-percenters patch?"

"They're an outlaw MC. They don't live by the laws of the country, they live and die by their own rules, make their money the less than legal way, and make no excuses for it."

Gillian glanced around her then taking in the clubhouse

backyard with fresh eyes. I waited for her to ask, and she did. "What about the Aces High MC?"

"They're kind of in between at the moment," I admitted.

"How can you be in between? I thought you either were or weren't."

"The Aces High MC have been moving toward going clean and totally legit for years. There are a few chapters who still dabble in less-than-legal things, but for the most part, they followed some pretty lucrative business plans Ghost's daughter gave them and now they're almost totally legit. This is the mother chapter of the club so while there's been a push to clean everyone up, we still dabble in support of other chapters, but our income is solely from the legit businesses."

"So, no running drugs or women?"

I shook my head then smiled at her. If she had added guns in that equation, I wasn't sure if I could be honest. "Don't get me wrong. These guys still ride free, live hard, and don't give a whole lot of fucks about the laws, but they don't need to bring in money in those ways." I grinned again. "We do have a few strip clubs, and one incredibly lucrative franchised bar and strip joint among the club."

"Franchised?" she questioned with a twinkle in her eye.

"Yeah, there are a pair of brothers in the Dakotas Chapter that started a place or took it over from someone. It's called Renegade Rosy's. Up there it's a strip joint. There's another one that opened down in South Carolina. Down there it's just a biker bar. They own other strip joints, but they are a mix of the usual place you might picture and a true-to-form gentleman's club. I heard that the guys down in Tallahassee are looking to start up a Rosy's of their own too."

"Do you guys have one here?"

"We sure do," I answered.

"Do women get naked there?"

I nodded my head to confirm it and then smiled at her. "They do, and they're all there of their own free will. They are also all screened for drugs, and no shady business goes on in the club. Hold 'Em, the guy who took Beth home, works over there. The guy is a freaking business genius or something. When he asked to look at Rosy's because business was shit at the one here in Cedar Falls, Ghost figured it couldn't hurt. He's turned it around in the six months he's been working over there."

"He's just a prospect though, right?"

"He is, but I have a feeling that Ghost sees what he needs to in him. That man is sharp."

"How do you know all of this? You just got patched in, isn't this stuff that you shouldn't know?"

"Nah. It's all spoken about commonly, and I talk about the club with Smoke when we're sitting around waiting on a call at the fire house."

She flicked the one-percenters patch on my kutte then, having been taking in everything there was to see as we talked. "So, if you're wearing this anyway, what was the real reason you didn't join the other MC?"

"There was also Kayla. I thought since her dad was reaching out to me, I could help her as much as she started to help me," I admitted.

"She helped you?" Gillian didn't even try to attempt to hide her skepticism and I didn't fault her for it.

"When I came back," I started but shook off where I was going with that. "I do have some PTSD issues since coming home from the Army. When I first came back though, it was not good. I had horrible nightmares. I would wake in a cold sweat, heart hammering, and screaming like a lunatic. She helped ease that when she first stayed over. I hadn't warned her, because I hadn't meant to fall asleep with her there. I guess I felt I owed her for helping me get through that. So, I stayed in California and then things were okay for a while. We were never in love passionately with one another – just comfortable."

"Then you moved here, and things went to shit?"

"No," I laughed as I explained. "Moving here was a symptom of how far things had already gone to shit," I explained. Gillie bit into that plump bottom lip of hers and I reached over to tug it out.

"A symptom?" she finally questioned.

"It started when we moved in together. She was okay at first, had just finished school, found a job in her field, and things were looking up. I was saving to buy a house, and then I wanted to get my bike, but didn't want to dip into that house savings." I didn't bother telling her about the college fund for my future children or my retirement plan. I wasn't going to scare her off with how far ahead I was planning for my future family. "I went to get a loan for the bike since it's a custom job and was kind of blown away when they told me I barely qualified because I had so much credit extended already. That's when I found out about all the credit cards she had taken in my name after she couldn't get any more in her own."

Gillian's hand came up to cover her mouth. "Are you kidding me?"

I shook my head, no. "I wish I was. I had to put a freeze on my credit after I bought that bike, and a good portion of my savings went to paying those credit cards off and getting rid of them. I took a major hit to my credit and to my bank account."

"You stayed though?" I could see the question in her eyes.

"You want to know why?" I took a swig of the beer I'd brought out with me and realized it had warmed up too much, so I put it aside. "I wish I could tell you. I was angry, no doubt. I felt like she just made a mistake and was still adjusting to not being daddy's little rich girl anymore, you know?" I laughed then. "Stupidly, I thought I could help her realize life wasn't about all those material things anyway. I thought I could show her that happiness came from other places."

"You were still trying to pay her back for helping you," Gillian muttered.

"Yeah, I guess I was." I explained to Gillian how I had ended up here. "You ever feel like you were stuck in the wrong situation too long, but being stuck there is what got you to where you needed to be?"

Gillian smiled knowingly at me then. "That's how I felt when I got settled in here. I love where I work, everyone at the station is awesome. Then there was Smoke, and the club, and being there that night for Beth. When I saw how the community pulled together to help her out, I knew I couldn't belong anywhere but here."

"You did that though," she argued.

"I got the ball rolling, but if I were back there, that ball would have fizzled out with maybe being able to guilt a few rich people into a couple tiny little checks to make them feel better about themselves. Here, the whole community pitched in to help out one of their own. I knew it didn't matter what I'd been through with Kayla at that point. I was home.

At first, I was going to hang in there and help her out until she was ready to leave, but I had no plans of going with her. Of course, somewhere along the way I met you and it became harder to keep that promise to myself. Then she fucked up and made it easier to let that promise go." I raised my hands in the air indicating everything around us. "Now, here we are."

"Now, here we are," she repeated before leaning in and pulling my face to hers. Once her lips touched mine, I felt it again. That zing of awareness. The chemistry that rocked through me and made me want to claim this woman in every way even when my brain was screaming 'it's too soon,'.

I pulled away from the kiss and looked Gillian in the eye. "You wanna get out of here?"

She laughed. "Isn't this your party?"

I grinned and shrugged my shoulders. "It's my party," I confirmed. "That just means I celebrate the way I want to."

"Fine then, let's get out of here. I'm assuming you have a room here somewhere?"

"I do tonight."

"Oh lord, what were they planning for you?"

"Well, prospects don't really get their choice of free pussy around the club. We have a hands-off policy so the night we're patched in, we're given a room to use as we see fit."

She scrunched her nose up at that admission.

"Even if you weren't here, that's not my scene. I'm sure some of the other guys would be all over it and most of the older ones probably were in their day."

"That's just..." I waited to see if she as going to tell me how disgusting things were, but Gillian surprised the shit out of me. "Probably the best present some of them could ever get," she finished while turning her gaze to Hatchet. He was a loner, nomad I'd come to know a bit better since he'd been here a couple weeks now. The man had not received his name because of his weapon of choice. His face had gone through some shit, and I hadn't bothered asking what happened, but he didn't seem to mind his moniker.

I laughed at Gillian before I stood and snatched her up over my shoulder. "Let's go, before you manage to insult some of my brothers."

We were on our way to the room I'd been given for the night, which meant carrying Gillian through the main party area. I received several offers from club girls as we passed to either join or ditch the outsider for them. Every last one of them got turned down. I noticed Gillian smacking one of their hands away when she tried to cop a feel of my abs. I spanked her ass as a thank you and continued right on to my room where I tossed her on the bed and locked the door behind me. By the time I turned back toward Gillian after locking the door, she was already half undressed.

"Better catch up, Surfer! Don't want to be late to your reward."

Holy Fuck!

I stood there, momentarily stunned, as Gillian peeled the rest of her clothes off and then sat up on the bed on her knees, fully nude, and beckoned me to her with a crook of her finger. "You're falling behind, soldier. What's a girl gotta do to finally see you naked?"

I glanced around. "Gillian?" I asked and received her laughter as answer.

She placed her hands on her shapely hips and grinned up at me, showing off her brilliant white teeth and the one that turned inward just a little proving that imperfections could be just as mesmerizing as their counterparts. "I have to be miss prim and proper at the hospital. I must be the perfect mom at the school. I have to be buttoned up and straight-laced in town. What I don't have to be is repressed in the bedroom. Now, get naked with me before I go pick one of those women out there and take them up on what they were offering." She winked at me then. "Someone's getting laid tonight. If It's not gonna be you, it's still gonna be me."

"Damn, Gillian!" I called out as I started stripping at record speed. I laid my kutte carefully across the back of the chair and then everything else was off in a flash and I was tackling little miss Gillian to the bed. That wasn't good enough for her sassy ass though. No. She needed to be taught a lesson. I flipped her over, yanked her hips up, smacked that ass, and sank two fingers home into her wet heat before she could get out the excited gasp that slipped from her lips.

"Yes, Gray," she called out as she leaned down some to give me the right angle. My thumb swept over her clit, teasing and tormenting her with light little wisps of movement before I plunged inside her heat once more, finding that spot that made her body sing, and pumping it hard with my fingers. Gillian creamed all over my hand, sending wetness dripping down her legs and my hand as she did so.

"You a squirter, babe?" I asked and was answered by a moan of appreciation. I smacked her ass then. "Asked a question, Gil. You squirt?"

"I never have before. Oh God!" She screamed out and I pumped my fingers in and out of her harder, not going gentle at all as I made sure to hit that sensitive spot inside of her. For my efforts I was rewarded with a stream of hot, sweet liquid gushing from between Gillian's legs.

"Oh God," she hissed again as another rush greeted me just in time for me to take my fill. I lapped up the liquid from her sex as she shook, and her inner walls convulsed around my fingers. I continued pumping, slower now, as she rode out the unexpected and explosive orgasm.

"Gillian?" I questioned. A small sound was all that returned. "You squirt, babe," I informed her. She started giggling then and flipped over causing my fingers to dislodge from her pussy as she did so.

"Holy shit, Gray. I've never felt anything like that before in my life."

"Good," was all I had to say before I pounced on her.

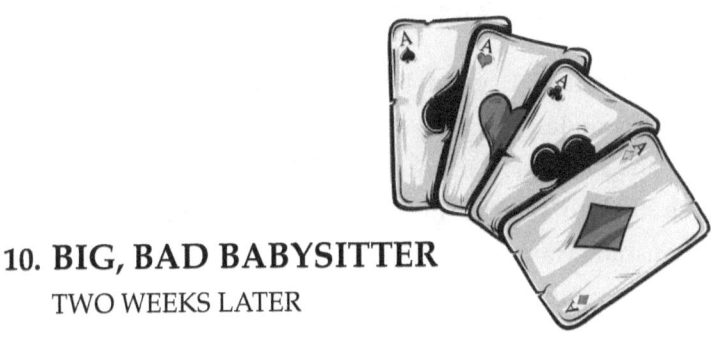

10. BIG, BAD BABYSITTER
TWO WEEKS LATER

BETWEEN MY JOB AND CLUB BULLSHIT I HADN'T HAD A SINGLE DAY off in the two weeks since I was officially patched into the MC. I was feeling it too. I always laughed before when I heard people use the term bone weary. I knew tired from when I was in the military, but I hadn't truly felt it again until now. I just wanted to collapse in bed for the rest of the day and do nothing else.

The minute my eyes closed my cell rang. I thought about simply not answering it, but I turned over and saw Beth's name there on the display. She rarely called. If anything, she sent text updates. I reached over and grabbed the phone. "Beth," I stated her name and waited for her to respond.

"No, I'm Beth," she teased.

I chuckled into the phone as I dipped my head back on to my pillow. "What's going on?"

"I wouldn't have called, but I can't find anyone else. I have a job interview in two hours, my babysitter has the flu, and Gillie's still on shift."

"On shift?" I asked before my brain could kick into working mode.

"She's a surgical nurse at CFH." I knew that. The fact that Beth had to remind me was a kick in the ass to how exhausted I was.

"Damn, okay," I managed to get out as I sat back up and threw my legs over the side of the bed. "I'm staying at Smoke's condo. Let me get you the address."

"Oh, that's good, I thought maybe you might have gone back to your girlfriend's house," she admitted.

"First, she's not my girlfriend." I shouldn't have to point this out to her. Didn't Gillian tell her that we were together? "Second, hell no I wouldn't go back to that house. Third, I'll watch Abby wherever you feel comfortable with me doing it. Smoke has a decent number of toys here for when his nephew comes over to hang out though, if that helps. If not, I don't mind heading your way."

"Crap, I'm so glad you mentioned a little boy. I almost forgot, Kade gets off the bus here in the afternoon. I should be back by then, but just in case, would you mind coming here?"

"I'll be there in ten minutes." I took my truck just in case I needed to take the kids anywhere in an emergency. By the time I got there Beth was in a frantic state.

"I'm so sorry to have to call you to babysit. I can't believe this happening. It figures, the one day I have an interview," she babbled on until I stopped her.

"Beth, seriously, it's no trouble. I wasn't working today. Everything is good here. You know I can handle emergencies if one crops up, and other than that, we're good. I promise.

Go to your interview and don't even give it a second thought, okay?"

She offered up a tight smile and looked away before I could see the moisture building in her eyes. At least, she thought she did. My heart went out to this woman. She had been through so much, and yet, she was still there fighting. Trying to get a job, do right by the daughter she had left, and feeling bad for getting help in doing that. Once she was out the door I turned to Abby.

"Momma's gone, let's party!" I put every bit of enthusiasm I had in me behind that and she giggled. "What do you say we drown ourselves in cookies and milk, play too hard, and then pass out for a nap?"

Giggles erupted from the tiny little girl once more before she came over and attached herself to my leg. I reached down and took hold of her pulling her up for cuddles. "Hey big girl, you been good for your mommy?"

She nodded her head vigorously in response as she stuck her three of her fingers in her mouth. I glanced around the house and took in the mess of pink and pastel toys that were lying around. I walked over to them and squatted near the baby dolls. "You like to play with the babies?" Again, more nodding as the slobber that was being produced from her sucking on her fingers started dripping down her arm and onto mine. "You have more teeth coming in, baby doll?" This time she just stared at me those wide eyes of hers. "Okay, well, let's see what we can do here," I explained as I set her down and sat my ass on the carpet. I could definitely handle emergencies just like I told Beth I could. What I wasn't sure about was how to entertain a toddler. I especially wasn't sure how to go about keeping a little girl entertained.

I picked up the doll and gave it a dubious look. The hair looked like a rat had nested in it. There was a distinct slash across the face from what appeared to be blue marker, and it was wearing a t-shirt on its arm, but otherwise unclothed. When I turned to glance back at Abby, she was quietly stacking blocks on top of one another. I tossed the doll behind me and moved to go help her build the best freakin' block tower there ever was.

The best freaking block tower ever lasted about two point five seconds before Abby Hulk-smashed it and joyfully cried out, "More!" We repeated this building and demolition process about a hundred more times before Kade was dropped off by the bus. I glanced worriedly at the clock because Beth had told me she should be back before he got home. Not that I minded looking after him too, but I wondered what was holding Beth up.

"It's you!" Kade shouted when he came through the door.

I grinned up at him. "What's up, little dude?"

Kade laughed as Abby knocked down another of my builds. "She managed to get you to build for her, huh? You know she can happily sit there and do that all day, right?"

I agreed with a tip of my chin and a sigh. "Dude, that was probably my best tower yet." Kade just chuckled.

"Where's Beth?"

"Not sure. She went to a job interview and hasn't been back yet." Kade's smile turned down almost immediately. "It's okay. She said she might not make it back before you got here," I explained even if that was stretching the truth a little. I watched as my words had the desired effect and his shoulders sagged noticeably in relief.

"How come your motorcycle isn't here?"

"Couldn't bring the bike in case there was an emergency. It's not that easy to strap you and Abby to my bike while we ride. The car seat alone would be tedious."

Kade laughed again. "I guess," he offered up and then started building the blocks up for Abby to knock down again.

"Do you have some homework or something you should be doing?"

Kade glanced over at me and then grinned. "Sure, but I'm helping you babysit instead. I can do that stuff later."

"Not sure your mom would think I did my job as a babysitter if you don't have your homework done. Don't want her thinking I'm not good enough."

He huffed. "Fine. I'll sit right there and do it while you build for Abby. My mom knows that I don't need a babysitter though. I'm almost a man," he boasted, and I had to look away so he wouldn't catch the grin on my face. Kade was five years old going on thirty according to his mom and I could see that. Though, there were times, like this where he showed a little more maturity.

We spent the next 45 minutes like that with Kade doing his homework while Abby fell asleep as she waited for me to build her another castle she could knock down. I was just about to go put Abby in her room for her nap when someone unlocked the front door and made their way inside. "Where is everyone?" I heard Gillian call out.

"In here," I managed to get out loud enough for her to

hear me, but hopefully not so loud that it woke Abby. Gillian's head popped around the corner a minute later along with a puzzled expression.

"What's going on, Gray?"

I quickly explained about Beth's interview and the sitter who canceled on her. "I'm worried. She said she would be back before Kade got here and that was nearly an hour ago."

"Okay, let's see," she offered and then sent out a call that was ignored. "Either she has her cell turned off or she just denied my call," Gillian explained as she sat with an exaggerate huff next to her son who had put away the work he was doing. A few minutes later the house phone rang.

I picked it up and immediately heard her. "It's Beth."

"Hey, what's going on?" I answered.

"I'm so sorry," she was all but sobbing into the phone as she got that out.

"Don't worry about it, and just tell me what has you so upset." Gillian moved closer so she could hear too without me having to put it on speaker phone and alerting either of the kids to Beth's distress.

"I had to sit there waiting for an hour just to get the interview with the pervert from hell who drooled over my boobs and forgot his questions in the middle of asking them because he was too preoccupied with my body," she spat out and I could hear the anger replacing whatever had made her cry. I was plotting the man's death, because it was starting to sound like it would be necessary.

"Then I decided that the job wouldn't be worth the trouble no matter the pay he offered, and I left. On the way back home I was going to stop at that little diner the kids like and get some take away for them so I wouldn't have to cook, and before I could pull into the place some asshole rammed into the rear end of my car. It jolted me into oncoming traffic, and..." her words were a blathering mess after that. I couldn't really make out what she was saying.

"Beth, you're going to have to slow down and take a breath, honey. I can't understand a thing you're saying right now."

"I'm so-so-sorry," she managed to sob out. "I didn't handle it well. The other cars stopped in time, but I was so shaken up. All I could think about was the other accident, and I kept having flashbacks of..." she cut herself off, but I could fill in the blanks. She was having flashbacks of waking to see her husband and child dead. I knew it because I still had nightmares occasionally about being there when that happened.

"They took me away in an ambulance and I don't know where my car is," she finally added. "Can you come get me?"

"I have the extra car seat in my car," Gillian offered.

"We'll be there as soon as we can, Beth. Just sit tight. I'll get everything straightened out for you."

"Thank you," she hung up just after those words were out of her mouth.

"Damn it, I hate this for her," Gillian lamented as she leaned over and tapped her son's leg. "Get your stuff together quietly while we get Abby to the car, baby."

"What's going on, mom? Is something wrong with Miss Beth?"

"She got in a little accident," Gillian admitted, and her

son paled immediately. "Nothing like the last one," she was quick to add.

"She wasn't hurt, was she?"

"No, but we have to go pick her up. I need you to get ready while we take care of Abby, okay?"

"Yeah, mom."

We were in Gillian's car with the two kids in back and headed to the hospital to get Beth when I dialed Smoke. He answered after the first ring.

"Yo!"

"Smoke," I called out and then filled him in on what had been happening today.

"Damn, Surfer, you are the poster child for why you're not supposed to take work home."

"I know, but this was the one necessary exception."

"I know it, brother, you need anything?" I'll get the boys in blue to release her car with no charge since none of it was her fault. Soon as I tell them whose car it is there won't be an issue anyway. I don't envy the jackass who rear-ended her though. No way he's getting out of that one now."

"Thanks dude, 'preciate it. Shoot me the address for the impound, and we'll head over after so I can drive it home for her."

"Nah, brother, take care of your people. I'll have the car there when you get back."

"Thanks. Hey, before you go, I hate to ask, but you know more people around here than I do. Beth went to an interview today. Guy was a creep who was talking to her chest instead of her face. You know anyone decent who is hiring?

She could use something. She was a stay-at-home mom before."

"I'll ask around the clubhouse and get back to you."

"Thanks," I told him before we both disconnected. Then Gillian, Kade, Abby, and me were off to go rescue Beth from her shit day. By the time we got back from picking her up the Prospect, Hold 'Em was there with Beth's car. He gave me a tight smile before pulling me to the side.

"I've got her, and the kid covered if you want to get your woman home." I took a long look at the man and then nodded my head. He had a fierce look in his eyes that wasn't going to take no for an answer, and I didn't quite understand why it was there. Still, I trusted him. He was one of the good ones. I was certain this was because he felt the way most of us did. Beth didn't deserve to have a shit day like she had today after everything she'd been through.

"Take care of her, call if you need me."

"Will do, Surfer." I shook my head and chuckled.

"Not gonna lie, that is taking some getting used to," I informed him. He just grinned.

"Yeah? Try gettin' your name turned into some fucked up pun just because those assholes saw you with a few girls."

I slapped him on the back and headed back over to Gillian's car. "Gonna follow you guys home and make sure you get there okay."

Gillian grinned at me. "You're leaving the hottie here with Beth? That's nice of you."

"What?" she winked at me and grinned then started backing out of the driveway. "See you at the house," she called off and waved. It did not take me long to hop into my truck and follow behind.

I was thinking on the way there that we would be putting Kade to bed sooner or later and then maybe we'd have some adult time. Instead, I was surprised to find a man sitting on the porch hanging out as if he belonged there. I parked the truck on the side of the road and immediately jogged over to Gillian's window. She looked pale and scared. "That's him," was all she said with a tip of the head toward Kade who had, luckily, fallen asleep in the car. What the fuck kind of timing did this douchebag have to show up now when things were just getting started with Gillian and me?

11. DADDY ISSUES

"What do you want to do here, baby?"

"I need for him to be gone and not cause a scene in front of Kade," she whispered to me as she picked up her cell phone. "I'm calling his mother to see what's going on. He shouldn't be here. He shouldn't even know where my house is."

I turned to see the man watching us, but not seeming bothered by anything that was going on or by the fact that we were basically ignoring him. I pulled my own cell out and let Ghost know that Gillian's ex happened to be a member of the Hell Hounds since he was wearing their kutte and that he was currently sitting his ass on her porch.

It only took a few minutes for Ghost and Smoke to come riding up alongside Wren. My brothers had not wasted any time in getting here. "What seems to be the problem here?" Ghost asked as he dismounted his bike.

The man on the steps just shrugged his shoulder. "No problem here. Just came to see my boy."

I laughed at that. "Yeah, for the first time? You just happened to stop by and see him out of the blue today?"

He smirked at me then. "What's it to you, pretty boy? My family is no concern of yours."

"It was my understanding you signed your rights away for the family you wanted instead. How'd that work out for ya?"

"You fuckin' prick!" He yelled before launching off of the porch and down into the yard. He seemed to have forgotten the other three men who were there in the wake of his anger. He quickly realized his mistake as he was hauled by two of them straight back into the shadows at the side of the house.

"Tell your woman to get the boy inside now, that way if he wakes, he won't have to see any of this," Ghost ordered, and I listened because it was sound advice. Once Gillian had Kade inside I came back around to find the man a little worse for wear.

"I don't know what fucked up game you're trying to play, but you will stay the fuck away from Gillian and Kade."

"You can't keep me from my son!" He shouted.

"You don't have a son, asshole. You traded him away for a piece of ass that didn't even stick around."

He hung his head then, and I could see the regret clear in the sag of his shoulders and the way his entire body seemed to wilt under that stance. "I just wanted to see my boy," he spoke quietly.

"Now ain't the time for that. You had a chance to be in his life. You shot that to shit. You made that decision. Now, you don't get to step foot into his life again. If, when he's an adult, he wants to find you then maybe you can try to explain why you thought it was better to give him up for some pussy. Right now, he's just a kid and he'll never understand."

Wren piped up then. "Fuck that, adult or not, no man who's a man will understand giving up a kid for pussy."

"I fucked up," he offered, and I thought I heard him sniffle. "I was young and stupid, and I fucked up."

"Yeah? And in all this time, in damn near six years, it never occurred to you before now that you fucked up?"

He glanced up at me then. Anger was starting to replace whatever misery he felt over not being able to see his kid. "She would have welcomed me back if you hadn't been here tonight."

I laughed, so did the other men. "She ain't stupid," I told him and left it at that. There really wasn't anything else to say. It didn't matter if I was there now or not, Gillian was an intelligent woman and she wasn't about to let a fool, who not only cheated on her while she was pregnant but ditched their kid for the other woman, back into her life. "Get gone, and don't think of showing here again. I find out you've come near either of them, and we'll do more than have words."

"Fuck you!" The asshole spat out as he moved toward his bike he had hidden off to the side of the house. "I'll get my boy back, and every one of you mother fuckers is gonna pay for this misstep tonight." The words flowed from his tongue as he took off on his bike. We allowed it, because there were neighbors taking peeks out of their windows.

"When there aren't so many witnesses around, we'll get that piece of shit taken care of," Ghost stated. I glanced at my three brothers. All of them were watching where the asshole disappeared to. "Put in a call tonight to the Hounds and let them know what just went down and that it won't be tolerated again," he told Wren.

"On it," Wren offered as he took off for his bike.

"You want someone here tonight to watch them?"

"No need," I explained to Smoke. "I'll be here."

"Figured you'd be staying over near Beth tonight since she had the day she did."

"Hold 'Em volunteered to stay with her earlier."

A look passed between Smoke and Ghost then. I wasn't sure what it meant, but I'd be talking to Smoke about it later.

"Gray?" Gillian's voice called out softly from the front door where she had it cracked open slightly.

"I'm coming," I called to her. "Thanks for showing so quick. I wasn't sure what exactly that was going to be about. Still not so sure it was about the kid."

"No thanks needed. That's what brothers are for. Go, take care of your woman." Ghost took off along with Wren then. Smoke glanced back at me and then smiled.

"She's like day to Kayla's night. Don't fuck that up." He tipped his head in the direction of Gillian.

"Don't plan to."

"I'll stop by and check in with Beth and see if she's okay with Hold 'Em there."

"Why wouldn't she be?"

Smoke looked at me oddly then. "She knows him well enough to have him at her place?"

I shrugged. "He's taken her home from the clubhouse before and she liked him well enough. Said he was funny."

"Think anything's going on there?"

"If you had asked me that question yesterday, I would have said no fuckin' way. After seeing the look in his eyes today, I don't know. I know he's soon to be a brother, but if he fucks with her head..."

Smoke held up a hand. "Say no more, I feel you. I'll have a chat with him tonight."

12. SECURITY DETAIL

CHURCH WAS PACKED THIS MORNING, AND IT WAS ALL DUE TO ME. Since I was only freshly made a member of this brotherhood, I worried that maybe this would be asking too much. Hell, I was still trying to wrap my head around how everything worked, and maybe I was still stuck in a little bit of the prospect mentality that none of this was really for me until I proved myself. The guys may have thought I proved myself, but I was still a bit unsure. It wasn't like me to be insecure at all, but damn if needing someone to have my back didn't put me on edge.

I glanced around the table seeing Ghost sitting front and center, leaned over discussing something with Hopper. Tuck was seated to his right and then around the table were Lou, Mick, Wren, Smoke, Chief, Bender, Crutch, and our prospect, Hold 'Em. I'd requested he be there even though he wasn't supposed to be until he was officially patched in. Fuck that though. The guy deserved his spot before I snuck in and took it first. Besides, I had a feeling he'd have a bit of an interest in what I was proposing here anyway. There were a few men missing, but Ghost told me that didn't matter. We had enough for a vote on something small.

I just hoped this was considered a small thing since it would inevitably involve the club as a whole, considering what went down to enable me to patch in early.

"Alright, settle down assholes. Our newest full member would like to ask something of us and we're going to hear him out this morning." Ghost turned things over to me then and everyone turned to face me.

"You all know about Beth," I started and got several smiles and nods in response. They all had grown fond of the woman and her kid over the past few months. "Well, I started seeing her friend, Gillian," I went on to explain only the fuckers couldn't just let that go.

"Hot piece of ass, man. Good on you," Tuck called out.

"Feisty too. You fuck up, I'm swooping in," Crutch called out.

"Shut the fuck up," Smoke broke in and put everyone in their place. "Anyone talked about your new woman like that you'd have a fist in your teeth. Now, listen up to what Surfer has to say."

I tipped my chin at Smoke who just sat there waiting. I was interrupting his day off with Poppy for this shit, and I knew it. "When I took her home last night her ex was waiting on her front porch." I gave them the brief run-down of why he was an ex and what he was supposedly doing there.

CHRISTINE MICHELLE

"That's pretty fucked up of him, but I'm not following with what that has to do with us?" Lou chimed in.

"He's one of the Hell's Hounds," I explained.

That revelation had everyone sitting a little straighter in their seats. "Beth's been bringing a Hound's woman 'round here?" Tuck asked.

I had to choke back the shit that wanted to spew out of my mouth. No need disrespecting a brother. "First, Gillian ain't his woman. I just fuckin' told you he left her 6 years ago for another chick who he married. Second, Gillian didn't even know he was part of the Hounds. He wasn't when they were together considering they were in high school together."

"Shit, sorry brother."

I waved him off even though my first inclination was to pop him in the fuckin' jaw. Didn't matter that he was older and a long-time member of the MC. I didn't like the fact that he'd just accused both Beth and Gillian of something, planting that thought in the minds of the men sitting around the table, even if that hadn't been his intent, the doubt would sit snugly in their minds.

"What is it you're wanting from us?" Ghost finally asked after everyone sat there quietly waiting.

"I want to have security on Gillian and Kade, possibly Beth when she's around them too. She watches Kade sometimes after school, and I'm worried this asshole will try to snatch the kid, especially after he found out I'm in Aces High and hanging around them."

"Look, no offense man, because I know you've gone

above and beyond for Beth since the accident, but neither of them is your old lady. Getting a poker run together to raise money for someone in need is one thing, putting a security detail on them is a different story. They ain't club affiliated," Lou explained and turned to Ghost for confirmation. When Ghost said nothing and continued to just watch me Lou carried on. "We can't get involved in shit like that when they ain't affiliated."

"The club already did, last night."

Ghost grinned then. I guess that was what he had been waiting for. "If you're willing to claim Gillian, she becomes our problem. Are you willing to claim her?"

"Yeah man, I'm willing to claim her and the kid." I made a point of adding Kade in there because wherever he went, he would have protection and that would extend to Beth when he was with her while his mom worked. I glanced over at Hold 'Em and he gave me a quick nod. Yeah, there was something I was going to have to talk over with him. It hadn't escaped my notice that Beth was a stunning woman in her own right. I just never felt that connection with her. Maybe it was because I had seen her in her worst moment and knew what that had looked like. I didn't know for sure; it just wasn't there for us like that. Knowing how Hold 'Em got his name though, I worried that he would be too much for her, or not enough, and she would end up with a whole handful of heartbreak all over again. I wanted nothing but the best for her and Abby moving forward, so I was going to have to see to that.

"That settled, we'll be looking out for Surfer's woman

and kid," Ghost told the men. A few smirks were passed around as if they knew that was how this whole meeting was going down before they were ever summoned in here. "Hope she's worth all this." Then Ghost pointed at Hold 'Em. "Now, for the next thing on the agenda." I turned to see the man in question pale slightly as he stepped forward with a question in his eyes. "This isn't how we normally do shit around here, as you know." He glanced in my direction. "Seeing as how you were here to witness Surfer's induction." He reached over on a counter where a box had been siting and opened it up. "Get your ass over here, man!"

Hold 'Em was quick to move to the club prez and then stood there sort of slack-jawed as Ghost presented him a kutte with his name on it and full top and bottom rockers that announced he was a full club brother of the Aces High Cedar Falls Chapter. "Shit!" Was the guy's only response before he took off the temporary kutte he had been wearing and exchanged it for the one Ghost held out to him.

"We'll be having a celebration and official ceremony later for you, but I thought you might have someone you want to claim yourself, and you can't do that without being a member." Hold 'Em glanced my way and then back to Ghost.

I didn't think he meant to be overheard, but I managed to pick up on his question to Ghost anyway. "You serious?"

"As a fuckin' heart attack, brother," Ghost boasted and then punched the guy in the chest, right over the embroidery on his kutte where his name was stitched in. "Welcome to the brotherhood, Hold 'Em." Ghost grinned out at everyone gathered around the table. "Before everyone congratulates our newest member, I think it's best we hear from him about who he's claiming as his woman."

There were a few curious glances around the table and then I noticed Smoke was watching me as Hold 'Em simply said, "Beth."

"Holy fuck!" One of the men swore under his breath. No one touched that subject though. Instead, they all started congratulating him. Once everyone was gone it was just Hold 'Em, Ghost, Smoke, and me in the room when I looked over at him and asked the question.

"Does she know?"

He shook his head. "She doesn't need to know yet. It isn't time."

"You just claimed her, man. You know even if she isn't aware, if she hears any stories later about what you did while you had that claim down..." I left it at that.

He narrowed his eyes at me. "You mind yours and I'll handle mine, brother. I know exactly what is at stake and the worth of everyone involved." I nodded to him and left to go break the news to Gillian that she was officially my old lady in the eyes of the club.

"We have to talk," I told Gillian after she invited me into her house that evening.

"Ugh," she groaned. "Worst words in the human language. I knew Joe was going to be an issue."

I grinned at her before taking her shoulders in my hands

and turning her to face me. She tried hiding behind the mess of wavy auburn curls she had obviously just taken down from the bun she usually wore to work. "It's not what you're thinking, I promise." I guided her to the sofa and waited for her to take a seat beside me.

"I did something today," I started, and she offered up a dubious look before attempting to scoot away. "Would you stop thinking the worst right off the bat?"

She gave me an apprehensive smile before responding. "I'll try, but it would be great if you would just get to it so my mind isn't wandering in all directions."

"How much do you know about biker culture?"

"About as much as I've seen on television in the approximately two point five episodes of that show I tried watching with Beth."

"Tried watching?"

She gave a sheepish little shrug. "I always fell asleep. My shifts are no joke sometimes."

"I get that," I told her.

"Yeah," she whispered. "I guess you do. I sometimes forget your job isn't to ride around looking sexier than hell on your motorcycle."

I laughed at that. "Sexier than hell, huh?"

She swatted at my chest. "We'll get to that. Right now, you need to tell me your news before I go back to guessing all the wrong things and jumping to outlandish conclusions."

"I claimed you today in front of the club," I told her, and she just stared at me with wide eyes but didn't say a thing.

"What exactly does that mean?"

"Your ex showed last night, and..."

She cut me off with yet another groan. "I knew this was going to be about Joe."

"No, listen. He happens to be in a rival club, one that isn't known for their tact or their impulse control. You've been around the bunch of bikers who are as close to the straight and narrow as most MCs get. The one your ex – Joe – is in, they are a different story, baby, and it ain't a good one."

"Well, that figures." Gillian blew out a breath of sheer frustration and then glanced back up into my eyes. "What does that have to do with what you're talking about? Claiming me?"

"You met Leanne before," I started to explain.

"Ghost's wife," she agreed.

"Yeah, Ghost's old lady. Claiming a woman in the MC is like making a statement that she belongs to only you. It's like a marriage or an engagement, or I don't know. I guess it's a little different to some people. It just means that we're serious about one another."

"Did you tell your biker boys that we're going steady, Gray?"

I laughed at that. "Yeah, babe. I told my biker boys that we're going steady. I know it's too soon for all that, but it had to be done in order to get security for you and Kade."

"Security?" Now, there was concern in her voice.

"I told you that your ex is in a rival MC. That's already no joke, but now he knows that he not only can get to you through your boy, but that his club can get to us through the both of you."

"You think he'd hurt us because I'm dating someone from a rival club?"

"I think he showed up here out of the blue after six years of no contact for a reason and he wasn't exactly surprised that an MC showed up to deal with him."

"Shit!" She was lost in thought for a moment, and I just let her be. No doubt, she needed time to process and me running my mouth at her while she attempted that probably wouldn't help. "So, what does this mean for me and Kade? You claimed me for security, but what does that mean?"

"When I can't be here, if I'm on shift or whatever, someone else from the club will be around to watch over the two of you. They don't have to disturb you, but they'll be around watching."

She shivered visibly. "That's really," she hesitated and then looked back up at me. "Intrusive."

"Better than coming home and having Kade snatched or worse."

"Can I think about this? It seems like a lot. How am I supposed to explain to Kade why all your buddies are suddenly hanging around?"

"You need to think about this?" I asked incredulously.

"Look at it from my perspective, Gray. Suddenly, my ex shows up out of the blue after six years making threats about wanting to see his son, and then I have to deal with a bunch of bikers hanging around to make sure my son isn't stolen from me by another biker gang that is probably up to no good and using my son and me as a means to get to you guys. Jesus."

"He's not with his ex-wife anymore. I have a feeling he would have been coming for you and Kade anyway." Again, I watched as she tried to shake off a violent shiver. "I know it seems out there, but do you really want to take the chance that he shows here when you're tired and getting off work? What about when Kade gets off the school bus at Beth's place?"

"Oh my God, do you think he would show up there? Beth would not handle that well."

"We have Beth covered too since Kade stays there." Beth was covered anyway since Hold 'Em had claimed her, but that wasn't my story to tell. Instead, I kept everything about Gillian and Kade.

She sighed heavily before crashing into me and just letting me hold her to my chest. "I promise, we'll get this shit straightened out as quickly as possible, babe. Then, if you don't want my claim on you, I'll remove it. Though, I really hope that isn't what you decide." Gillian's cell phone rang, and she looked like she was going to ignore it until she saw who was calling.

"Hello?" she asked as she answered the phone and then quickly put it on speakerphone while putting a finger to her lips indicating I should remain quiet.

"Gillian?" There was a pause. "Good, I was worried that I would miss you again." Apparently, Gillian had been dodging this woman's calls. "I wanted to talk to you about Joe. He says he went to see you both the other night," it was clear the woman was happy about that fact. "Though he did mention he wasn't really able to see Kade. I can understand your hesitation, but honey, he's finally realized what a huge mistake he made. He even went so far as to buy me a new car so that I would have a safer, roomier ride for when Kade stays with me."

"Joanne, he does not have any rights to see Kade. He signed them away in order to marry his wife, remember?"

"Psh, they're divorced now, honey. Things can go back to the way they should have been," the woman cooed.

"And how exactly should they have been?"

"Well, isn't that obvious? The two of you were always beautiful together. The three of you could be a family now. I know it's too early to think about that, but at the very least Kade deserves to know his father."

"Joanne, quit dreaming. Kade deserved to know his father from the time he was born, but his father tossed him out like yesterday's garbage right along with me. What on Earth would make you think that I would ever give that man another chance in either of our lives? What happens the next time Joe decides that he wants another woman who won't tolerate him having a kid? My son is old enough to feel that pain now. He's old enough to know that his father is choosing someone else."

"He wouldn't do that again," she insisted.

"I bet you never thought he'd do it the first time since you raised him on your own and he knew how hard it was to be a single mother, right?"

"Well," she started to say.

"Yeah, but he did it to me and to Kade anyway. He left us on our own for the five years since I had Kade and most of my pregnancy before that. I will not put myself or my son through that again. If you are going to be helping Joe see Kade behind my back, then I will be forced to stop your access to my son as well."

"Gillian!" The woman cried out in shock. "You can't do that. He's my grandson."

"If you're willing to go against my wishes where Joe is concerned then I absolute can and will do that."

"Joe is his father, he has rights!"

"Joe is not his father. He's nothing more than a sperm donor, and he doesn't have any rights because he gladly signed them away. I'm done with this conversation tonight."

Gillian disconnected the phone before Joe's mother could get another word in. "Well, it's sounding more and more like I have to take you up on your offer. She's going to push it. She won't take kindly to having her access to Kade cut off after all these years. I don't know what I'm supposed to do now, though. When Beth gets a job, I won't have someone for those times to watch out for Kade. It was supposed to be Joanne since she's retired, but now..."

I leaned in and kissed the top of her head, squeezing her to me a little tighter. "We'll come up with something. I'll ask around at the club and see what the women do with their children, okay? Maybe they have an in with an after-school program or something."

"Why did he have to come back?" Her words were choked out with emotion, and I wanted nothing more than to make the asshole disappear for causing her any pain at all, but also for making it resurface when she thought she had her life figured out.

"I don't know, baby, but I promise you we will get that shit under wraps quick. What do you say we go get busy making some dinner for little man so you can keep things normal for him? Plenty of time to fall apart with me behind closed doors later, yeah?"

She glanced up at me then, glassy eyes wide in surprise. "I'm not so sure it's a good idea for you to be staying over just yet. I don't want Kade to..." her words cut off just as the boy came bounding into the room.

"Mom, what's we eating for dinner?"

Gillian hid her face a minute so she could clear the tears from her eyes. "Dude, we were just discussing what we thought you might want to eat," I lied.

The kid waved me off with the flip of his hand. "That's easy. Mac-n-cheese, dude."

I chuckled and felt Gillian do the same where she was still wrapped in my arms. "Why don't you go finish up any homework and we'll get that ready for you?" she finally called out.

Kade stood there for a minute and then smiled at me. "Can Gray sleep over so I can show him my new game?"

I pulled my lips tight against my teeth to keep from laughing since Gillian had just been worried about how her son would react to me being here all night. "I'm sure we can work something out, bud," she told him, and he took that as a yes and ran off before any further discussion could be had. She glanced up at me then, as if remembering something. "Shit! I'm supposed to cover for Bethany tonight. I forgot all about it with everything going on. It's not an all-night thing, just a few hours. This is the night when they do the extended hours for people who can't make it in due to work or whatever."

"It's all good. How about you go get ready, I'll get dinner

made, and then I'll stay with Kade tonight. I'll take him by the station to see the engine, if that's all right with you?"

"You are a lifesaver, Gray."

Once she was off and getting ready, I started making dinner while also making shooting texts to the guys to make sure she would be covered while at work. "Can I help?" I turned to see Kade standing there watching me.

"Sure, dude, grab that chair and get on over here." I had already strained the noodles so all that was left was to add the powdered cheese, butter, and milk to his mac-n-cheese. The hot dogs were already cooked up and I had found some buns in the cabinet. "You like buns for your dog, or you just eat them plain?"

He shrugged his shoulders as I handed him the measured-out milk to dump in. "Sometimes I like the buns."

"Is today one of those sometimes days, or you just want the dog on the plate?"

"How are you eating it?"

"I'm tossing mine on the bun, little man."

"I want a bun too."

"All right," I told him and then handed him the large spoon to stir with. "Now, put some muscle into that so all the cheese gets stirred in right."

"I'm strong enough," he informed me then started to stir while poking his tongue out of the corner of his mouth as if it helped with the effort. I turned to see Gillian standing in the entryway to her kitchen smiling at us. She was wearing a set of mint green scrubs and with white Crocs on her feet. I raised an eyebrow in question.

"They might just be the ugliest shoes ever, but when

you're on your feet all day and dealing with spills sometimes too, they're the best things ever."

"Whatever you say. Do you have time to eat this gourmet meal with us?"

She shook her head. "I'll grab a dog to go on a bun with ketchup."

"Ketchup?" she nodded and Kade laughed. "Seriously, that's the only thing you want on the bun with your dog?"

"Seriously," she informed me. "I hate mustard."

"What about relish?"

"Pickles belong on the side of your plate when you order a sandwich in a restaurant, because they make lovely decorations."

"Damn, I think I just found the relationship deal breaker," I stated in disappointment as I threw my hand over my chest to protect my heart. Then I looked to Kade. "Don't worry little dude, I'll teach you the fine art of eating manly man dogs since your mom is just a girl and only wants ketchup." That had Kade giggling hysterically. Gillian gave me her narrow-eyed disapproval and then she swooped in and gave her son a kiss and turned to offer the same to me.

"I'll be home by ten o'clock. Try not to turn Kade into too much of a man just yet. I'd miss him when he has to move out on his own and pay his own bills and stuff," she teased.

"Nuh-uh. I'm no dummy. I'm livin' with my momma forever."

"Wait until you hit puberty kid, you'll change your mind on that."

"What's pubity?"

"Nothing we need to worry about just yet. Be good for

Gray, and don't try to lie about your bedtime. In bed, under the blankets, and eyes closed by eight tonight."

"Yes ma'am," he offered with a little whine to his voice. I turned and winked at her then repeating his, "Yes ma'am," with a promising tone to my voice.

We finished up, ate, and then cleaned up our mess after Gillian left. Then I swooped Kade up and took him to get his shoes on. "Let's go take a look at the fire trucks, little dude."

13. BABY MAMA DRAMA

Luckily the engines were parked in the station garage when we got there, and I was able to get Smoke to come out and help me show Kade around everything. A few of the other guys got in on the act too even going so far as to stick him into his own boots and turnout jacket. I took a couple pictures with my phone because I knew that Gillian would love to see her little man dressed up as a firefighter in gear that swallowed him up and showed he was still very much her little boy.

"Gray," I heard called out and turned to see Kayla prancing into the open garage bay as if she were right at home here.

I glared as I answered. "What are you doing here?"

"I came to see you, baby," she cooed as she glanced around and realized who the kid was that I had with me. Her eyes narrowed and then she turned back to me instantly making them big and wide. "I didn't realize you were having another charity event."

"You need to get gone, now!"

"Hey Kade, what do you say we go check out the bunkhouse where me and the guys sleep when we're not busy fighting fires."

"Yeah!" Kade hollered with a fist pump. "You coming, Gray?"

I turned to Kade and smiled at him. "I have to clean this mess up first, and then I'll be right in to show you where I sleep when I'm here too." His eyes went wider. "You sleep here too?"

"Sometimes, little dude. Go on with Smoke for now, I'll be right in." Smoke got him the hell out of there while a couple other guys started clearing the mess that they had dragged out for Kade to play with. While I had my eyes on them Kayla moved in closer, too close. I went to take a step back, but the damn woman launched herself at me and tried for a kiss. I moved my face so all she got was my stubble-roughened cheek. I took hold of her arms and forcibly moved her back away from me and as I took a step back from her, I noticed Gillian headed our way.

I didn't even know how to feel in that moment except murderous towards Kayla. If she'd just fucked shit up for Gillian and me, I would have her on a plane back to Cali before she was able to even think about what to wear for grand re-arrival.

Gillian didn't seem phased which made me think she saw more of that little show than I was aware of. She marched right over to me and tossed her arm around my waist, leaning up to get a kiss that I had to bend to give.

Yeah, she was showing Kayla what it looked like when the man was interested in giving that welcome kiss.

"You're fuckin' her now?" Kayla started shouting. "Let me guess, you were already fuckin' her before we split up? That's it isn't it? You were cheating on me with that skank. She can't be attractive anymore. Look at her, she already shit out a kid. I bet she has nasty stretch marks, and saggy tits that need a special support bra to stand up right."

I just stared at Kayla for a moment as I let all her vitriol settle in. Then I moved to push Gillian a little further to my back in case Kayla tried some stupid shit. Gillian wasn't having it though. "Unlike you, Gray doesn't have to cheat. He has what everyone else around here might consider great character. You were found cheating though, with one of his brothers. If that didn't clue you in that thing were over between you two, I don't know what should. As for my body, Gray likes it just fine, sweetheart, because it doesn't come attached to crazy."

Kayla huffed as some of the men still gathered around laughed at her. "We can definitely say I traded up in all aspects, and now that it's pretty obvious you aren't welcome here, you can get gone."

"Gray," she pouted.

"Oh, I'm sorry, did you not hit up the station to see if any of the men here needed their cocks sucked behind my back too? It won't matter now. Suck away, because you are nothing to me."

"That's not a very nice way to talk about the mother of your child," she stated evenly.

Gillian gasped at that and glanced up at me. I shook my

head, because I knew what she was asking. Did I have a kid that I wasn't caring for?

"We don't have any kids, Kay."

"Not yet, but in about six months," she said as she patted her very flat stomach.

"Well, let me know when your next appointment is then so I can go too and ask the doc how soon a DNA test can be done."

"As if it could be anyone else's?" she gasped out indignantly.

"I caught you in the clubhouse, in front of a room full of people, with a dick in your mouth that wasn't mine. We barely even had sex the past few months when we were together because I was to the point where I couldn't stand lookin' at you, let alone be able to get it up for you. So, yeah, if you really are pregnant, chances are pretty fuckin' favorable that it's not mine. If it is, you best believe I'll be going for full custody. We'll worry about that after you prove you're even pregnant and a DNA test confirms paternity though."

Kayla turned on her heel and started stomping away, but once she got to the edge of the garage where the bay doors were still left open, she glanced back with her parting shot. "I'll send you the appointment information tomorrow."

"She can't be serious?" Gillian questioned once Kayla was gone.

"I think she thinks she's being serious," I informed her. "Listen, I know this hard to hear, but I want you to know a few things. First, I was never with her without a condom. We were together for two years, it never occurred to me to not use them. I'm guessing at least part of my brain was in working order and didn't trust her. Second, I can count on one hand the number of times we had sex in the past four months before we went our separate ways and I'd still have fingers left over. Third, I was tested after I split with her anyway, just in case. The chances she could be carrying my baby are almost nil."

"There is a chance though," she whispered.

"If the fates are willing to be so unkind, yeah, I guess there's a slim chance if she's saying she's three months along already. It would have to be a hell of a fuckin' miracle though with her on the pill, using condoms, and only having gone at it once in that time frame."

"Can I just say that I will stand by you no matter what, but I really hope it isn't true."

"You and me both, babe."

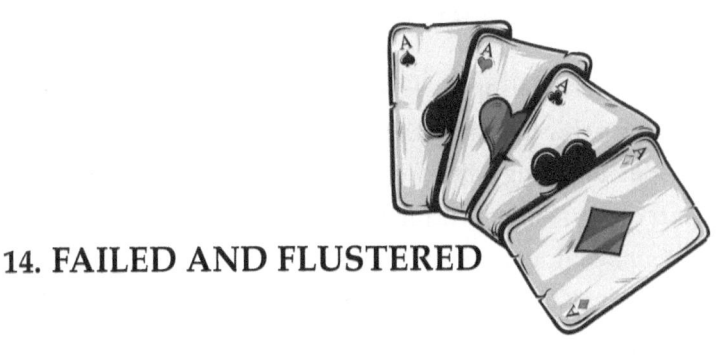

14. FAILED AND FLUSTERED

"I REALLY HATE THAT YOU HAVE TO GO DO THIS TODAY," GILLIAN told me as she leaned in and placed a sweet kiss on my neck.

"Me too. I honestly don't think there's anything to worry about though."

"What if it's true though? I have to say I'm a little worried about what the fallout will be like."

"Gillian, you don't have a thing to worry about. If it turns out she's pregnant, and that it is somehow my kid, then we will work through it. I'm not giving you up. There's no way in hell I'd go back to her even if you left me. I'll be leaving that office and going directly to a lawyer's office to have them draw up paperwork for her to relinquish custody. If you don't think you can handle a man with another woman's kid, then..."

"Are you kidding me? You've basically stepped in and become the man in Kade's life. What kind of a person would I be if I turned you away or your child?"

I shrugged my shoulders. "Things are a little different in

my case considering Kade's already in school. This will be bringing a tiny baby into the mix."

"I'm not going anywhere, Gray. If there's a baby, it will be a part of you. I'm not turning any part of you away."

I smiled down at her. "Good to know. I better get going," I told her as I glanced down at the time on my cell phone. "I'm hoping the quicker I get there the faster this is over with."

"Ride safe," she whispered in my ear before kissing the side of my face and backing away.

"Always do, baby. I'll call you the minute I know."

KAYLA WAS WAITING OUTSIDE of the doctor's office when I pulled in and parked my bike in a curb-side spot near the door. "It's about time you got here," she huffed. "What if I miss my appointment because you couldn't be on time?"

I pulled my phone out of my pocket and glanced down at the time. "There's still 15 minutes before your appointment starts," I inform her.

"They said I needed to be at least 20 minutes early to fill out paperwork."

"Then what the fuck are you doing standing around out here? You have two legs that could have walked your ass inside so you could have been doing that instead of wasting everyone's time."

"Ugh!" She growled out as she turned on her heel and marched attitude first into the office. I kind of felt bad for the staff since I just put her in a mood that I knew she wouldn't crawl back out of easily. Still, I wasn't about to take the blame for her bullshit, nor was I going to allow her to postpone this little visit any longer because she didn't make it to the appointment on time. Fuck that. I didn't want to be left waiting on eggshells to find out, one way or another, and I was certain Gillian didn't either.

Kayla was seated and filling out the forms when I finally made it inside. I chose to sit on the opposite side of the room from her. I didn't need her needling me the entire time we had to wait. She glanced up and glared at me for a few minutes. "Seriously, Gray?"

"You got something to do there?" I tipped my head to indicate the clipboard full of paperwork she was supposed to be filling out.

"Asshole," I heard her grumble and a woman sitting to my left gave me a sheepish smile and then hid her face with her hair, trying not to laugh.

We sat there in the office for a full ten minutes past the time when Kayla turned those forms in. When we were finally called back, I had to wait through the process of watching Kayla getting weighed and bashfully crying, "Don't look, Gray."

"Like I give a fuck what your weight is," I managed to get out around an exasperated sigh. "We aren't together. I don't care. If you're pregnant, I'll care for the baby that you're gaining like you're supposed to be, but not a bit about your end of shit."

The nurse gasped as if I was a monster. "If you only knew," I told her. "Chances are astronomical that if she's pregnant, it ain't mine." The nurse's eyes grew wide with my admission, but she kept her silence as she showed us to the room. The nurse left me to wait in the exam room while she took Kayla for a urine and blood sample.

"Was that really necessary?" Kayla snapped as soon as the door closed behind her when she was done.

"In light of your dramatics out there, yes." She huffed. Of course, she huffed, as if she hadn't put us right here in this position with me hating her and the fits she threw when she didn't get her way.

"I'm going to need you to leave that whore of yours behind once the baby gets here so get it all out of your system now. Once she's here I'm not sharing you with anyone," she demands.

I just took in all that she was for a moment before speaking. "Won't you be sharing me with the baby?"

Her lip curled up in a snarl. "No, I won't. The kid is going to have a nanny because I will have earned my inheritance by the time she's here."

"The kid? A nanny? Do you even understand how much of a cunt you are when you speak?"

"What? You expect me to raise it, or to have to lose precious time with my love because it shit it's pants again?" Her nose was scrunched up in disgust. "No way. I'm doing this for you because I know you'd hate me if I got rid of it."

Not fuckin' likely at this point. I had never wondered about nature versus nurture before, but if a child of mine were born to her, I would be worried every day of their lives that they would turn out like this and I didn't think I could stomach it. I didn't bother saying that out loud. The fact was,

I had been recording our conversation anyway, to play later, just in case she was pregnant with my kid.

"So, you're having this kid because you think it's the only way to get me back, yet you don't plan on helping with it once it's here? And you think your plan is going to make me stick it out with you?"

She gave me a 'duh' look and when I waited for a response she sighed dramatically before answering. "Obviously, it will be on you to care for it, and the nanny. I'm going to be too busy for that stuff. Besides, you know I'm not cut out for it. And yes, you will be with me because you would hate to think of what might happen to it if you aren't around. I'll be more careful in the future about birth control, so this never happens again. One kid should be enough for you, right?"

I was sending this recording to her father. Something needed to be done about this woman. She wasn't right in the head, and I was kicking myself in the ass for having thought it wasn't quite this bad for so long. Before I could respond to her craziness there was a knock on the door. The person entered and gave Kayla an odd look as she did so.

"Hello," she offered as she glanced between the two of us. "I'm Dr. Carmichael." She turned her focus solely to Kayla then. "I understand you came in saying you thought you were several months along in a pregnancy and just needed to confirm and get established for care?"

"That's what I told the nurse," Kayla snapped at the woman. "Why must I constantly repeat myself?"

If I could strangle her, I would be granting mercy on the people of the world who would be saved from interacting with her. I should be hailed a hero for it, actually. I was pretty sure this doctor would thank me, at the very least. The woman speaking again snapped me out of some pretty vivid fantasies I was beginning to have of my hands around Kayla's throat.

"Yes, well, I just wanted to verify that was the case because the results are pretty conclusive. Is there a reason you thought you might be pregnant and so far along?"

"I haven't had a period in over three months, my breasts are aching all the time, and I'm unable to sleep. My moods are all over the place, certain foods turn my stomach, and I've been sick a lot."

"Vomiting?" The doctor tried to clarify.

"What the fuck else do you think, 'I've been sick a lot' means?" Kayla asked snidely.

The doctor glanced at me again and gave me the most brilliant smile ever before turning back to Kayla and getting down to business. "Well, Kayla, first I need to inform you that I will not take on abusive clients so after this visit you will have to find a new doctor. Secondly, the tests prove conclusively that you are not pregnant. Thirdly, if what you are saying about your symptoms is true then I suggest finding another doctor quickly so they can address what might be wrong with you."

I stood and held my hand out to the woman. "Thanks a bunch, Doc. You just made my year." She grinned quickly before covering it and putting her neutral professional face back together.

"What? Gray, where are you going? You heard her; I could be dying."

"Yeah, well, a kid may have been my problem. Whatever you have going on isn't. I've been tested so I know I didn't pick up anything nasty from you. Probably for the best I never went ungloved there."

"You're just going to leave me here like this after I received news like that?"

"You ran up credit card debt in my name, dragged me here to be your slave and fix up a house you inherited that I gain nothing from helping with, and then you added insult to injury when you got down on your knees in the middle of my clubhouse and sucked one of the out-of-town brothers off in front of everyone. I'm thinking your karmic justice is due and maybe it's about to pay off in spades."

"Gray, I know you aren't a heartless bastard," she snipped.

"No, but you are, so thanks for teaching me how that's done."

With that, I turned and left the room. The office and the people in it blazed by me as I moved with a purpose to get out of the building and inhale some fresh fucking air that tasted like pure freedom. The rumble of my Triumph as I started it up was sweet fuckin' heaven and the open road on the way back to a woman who is the opposite of the one I just left behind – bliss. Pure bliss.

"Gray?" I could read her lips as Gillian called out to me from her front step before I killed the engine. The worry in her eyes was evident, and I didn't want her to have to wait any longer with that weight on her shoulders, so I grinned over at her and shook my head in the negative. Her eyes grew larger in surprise, clearly having expected the worst.

I dismounted the bike and left my helmet hanging from the handlebar before making my way to my woman and picking her up in my arms, swinging her around, and then planting a giant kiss on her. "Yeah, baby, we're celebrating tonight. Nothing left to tie me to that crazy bitch."

"So, it was all a lie?"

"Let's go inside and I'll fill you in."

"Beth's here too," she warned. "I was too nervous to wait alone."

I smiled at her and pulled her in for one more kiss. "That's okay, baby. I get it. Kind of wish I'd had someone to hold my hand for the wait while I was there," I offered up with a laugh. "That shit was crazy, brutal, and thank fuck it turned out in my favor."

Once we were all situated in Gillian's living room the girls both watched me for a moment before anyone spoke. "I'll be honest you look like an entirely different person than the one I saw last night," Gillian mentioned.

"Freedom must look good on me," I offered with a chuckle before telling them in detail about what happened.

"I just find it so hard to believe that she would say something like that," Beth finally told me when I was done.

I figured no one would believe me when I told them how crazy she was. I took a recorder along with me just to be sure I had it all down in case she was pregnant, and I needed it to take to court with me. I hit play on the little audio recorder

I'd picked up for the occasion. I hadn't wanted to bog my phone down with possibly an hour or more of conversation, but the recorder supposedly could hold over 500 hours of audio recording.

"Jesus," Gillian hissed.

"Not that I doubted you were telling the truth, but she really said those things. She opened her mouth up and allowed those words to come spilling out and had no remorse about it. I just heard it with my own ears and I still can't wrap my head around it." Beth stood and moved toward the kitchen. "I'm grabbing a drink, anyone else want anything?"

"Can you grab me a water?" Gillian asked her and then turned to me. "What about you, babe? Need anything?"

I smiled at her as I shook my head to let Beth know she was safe to head on in after their drinks. "Just you, G."

"G?" she laughed.

I shrugged my shoulders. "Not a fan of Gillie-bean. Makes you sound like you're 12-years-old."

Her answering grin told me a lot about how she felt about the nickname. "Honestly? I hate that nickname, but I can't say no to her," she tipped her head in the direction of where Beth had gone in the kitchen.

"I get that. I have trouble saying no to her too. Not sure if I ever believed in a God, but seeing bad shit happen to someone like her really makes me question how there could be one out there."

"Sometimes, I think other people's karma kicks the wrong ones in the ass inadvertently."

My brows furrowed in as I took in her words. "Her man?"

She nodded. "We can talk about that later, but he was a bit of a shit."

That took me aback. All this time I'd been thinking that Beth had lost the love of her life in that wreck. It never occurred to me that maybe she hadn't been happy before either. "We'll definitely talk about that later."

"Talk about what?" Beth asked as she walked back into the room to hand Gillian her water.

"Do you really want to know?" I asked the question with a suggestive wiggle of my eyebrows, and she cringed.

"Nope, I sure don't. You keep your adult, couple time to yourselves." Her lip poked out in a bit of a pout as she made the statement. "I kind forgot what it's like to do adult things other than pay bills and play momma to Abby."

I glanced at Gillian, and she smiled sweetly at Beth. "We'll do a girl's night real soon."

"I'm sure there are a few old ladies from the club who would love to get in on that action too," I informed them.

"Oh! Yes! We have to invite Leanne, she's a hoot!" Beth was suddenly full of so much giddy excitement that she literally bounced her bottom on the chair and squealed like a schoolgirl getting ready for a slumber party. The front door opened before the women could start planning anything and Kade came bouncing into the house.

"Hey Ms. Beth!" He shouted when he saw her. Then he noticed me sitting with Gillian on the couch. "Hey, Gray! I didn't know you were coming over." His excitement to see me was contagious as he managed to take my full attention away from everything else.

"Sure, little dude. Someone had to make sure you were

doing your homework when you got here," I told him and offered up a quick wink.

He sighed, but then grinned at me. "You know I'm too smart for that stuff, right?"

"Of course, you are, but sometimes you have to play the game. Let everyone see how brilliant you are so they stop riding your back."

"Huh." He appeared thoughtful for a moment before he grinned again. "I bet you're right. Our teacher never yells at all the smart kids who turn in their homework."

"She probably doesn't watch them as closely either, and you know what that means?"

He was hanging on with bated breath as he shook his head in the negative. "No. What?"

"It means they don't get caught doing things that the other kids get caught doing."

"Aww, man! Why didn't I think of that? Thanks, Gray!" Kade slung his backpack back up on his shoulder and started heading for the kitchen.

"Where are you going? Don't I even get a hello?" Gillian asked the boy's back as he shot through the room with a purpose.

"Sorry. Hey, mom! I'm going to get my homework done first, then I'll tell you all about my day." He grinned, winked at me, and then turned into the kitchen.

"I don't know if that was the best advice in the world you gave him or the worst, Gray."

"Probably a mixed bag, depending on what he's trying to get away with at school." Both Gillian and Beth laughed.

"When Abby's older and refusing to do homework, I'm

going to remember this moment. Creative parenting sounds like it's right up my ally."

I must not have schooled the question in my eyes before she noticed. I was wondering how she hadn't already experienced school-aged parenting considering the two kids who had died in the car accident with her husband.

"They weren't my children, and they had only recently come to live with us. They were Michael's kids from his previous marriage. Their mom barely let us see them when he and I started dating. Then suddenly out of the blue, three years later, there she was dropping them off on the doorstep with a bag each and telling us they were our problems now."

"What the fuck?" I asked, feeling strange at finding out all the things about Beth's life before the accident that were so contrary to how I had been picturing them.

"I don't remember seeing another woman there at the cemetery that would have been their mom. She would have sat up front with you, right?"

Beth shrugged; her eyes downcast toward her feet. "She never came back for the funeral. She had a lawyer request their death certificates so she could collect some insurance money off their life insurance her mom had gotten in their names. They didn't even offer to help with funeral expenses. She was in Europe when the accident happened. I guess that's why she dropped the kids off with us. She's a groupie or something for some rock band and got the chance to go on tour with them, but of course, she couldn't bring kids along." Beth shook her head. "They were sweet kids, and I will never understand how they turned out the way they did with the parents they had," she was muttering the words by the time she finished speaking as if she had just been thinking out loud without realizing it.

"I better get going soon. Abby's going to need dinner in about an hour and I'm already going to regret allowing her to nap this long." Beth stood and looked between the two of us before she turned and walked toward the kitchen. "How about I take Kade with us and give you guys the night to celebrate your good news?"

"But you have celebrating to do too with the new job," Gillian argued.

Beth turned around and grinned. "I'll get my celebrating in during our girl's night."

"Where are you working?"

"Hold 'Em came by earlier to tell me that a position opened at the pawn shop the club has. He says there's plenty of security and I'll be working the front desk and doing payroll and stuff since the girl they had doing it quit last week."

I was pretty sure Hold 'Em had been banging the girl who quit not too long ago. I was going to have to reiterate to him that Beth wasn't one of those quick one and done flings and that she needed the work. Not that I thought he'd purposely fuck Beth over, but just to err on the side of caution. She didn't need any more grief in her life.

"I'll go get a bag ready for Kade. Are you sure you're okay with seeing him off to school in the morning? If not, I can set an alarm and make sure..."

"I promise, I have it under control. Everything will be fine. You guys enjoy your night." In under twenty minutes the house was quiet and there was just Gillian and me occupying it.

"I'd like to ask if you want to help me make dinner, but honestly I'm not even the least bit hungry for food right now," she finally said, breaking the silence.

I didn't bother responding. Instead, I leaned in, snatched her up and over my shoulder and headed for her bedroom. Once we were in there, I tossed her ass on the bed and watched her bounce a bit, tits jiggling as she did, before I finally gave her an order. "Strip!"

"Yes, sir!" My dick kicked up to full attention after hearing her response and seeing how quickly she followed my command. Her shirt went flying and knocked over a lamp that was on the bed side table. Then her bra joined it. Her tits continued to jiggle deliciously as she maneuvered herself into a position where she was able to pull her pants free of her sexy, smooth legs.

"Mmm, I love these sexy legs of yours, baby."

"I bet you'll love them even more when they're wrapped around you as you pump your hard cock into me."

"Jesus, fuck! G, I love your dirty fuckin' mouth," I told her just before I claimed that mouth with my own. I didn't have it in me to go gentle with her and once we were undressed enough, I bent her over the bed and mounted that sweet ass of hers.

"Yes, Gray! Fuck me hard, honey. I need it!"

That was all the invitation I needed. I sank balls-deep right into my woman's sweet, tight pussy. "Fuckin' heaven, baby."

As we lie there with her head on my chest and my fingers combing through sweat-slick hair she sighed and then shimmied even closer to me so that her front was pressed to my side. "Gray?"

"Yeah, baby?"

"Remember how you said that if things were straightened out with Joe you could always remove your claim on me if I wanted you to?"

I stiffened beneath her almost afraid to hear what was coming. "Of course," I answered even though I wasn't sure hearing those words would ever be something I was prepared for.

"I don't want you to do that," she admitted on a whisper.

"You don't?" I turned my head, craning my neck so I could look down into her eyes, but they were downcast. I reached down, lifting her chin with the fingers of my right hand since she was curled up in my left. "You don't want me to release my claim?"

She shook her head gently against my chest and I thought I felt some moisture accruing there. "I'll understand if you aren't ready for something of that level considering everything that happened with your ex-girlfriend, but I don't see myself ever wanting to walk away from you."

"Well, that's good baby, because I definitely have no plans to walk away from you. Hell, I wasn't sure how I was supposed to handle it if you told me you wanted it the other way. There was this plan to get you to see things my way, and..."

"Shut up," she said through a small fit of giggles as she snuggled closer and placed a quick kiss on my chest. "I'm not sure we're ready for Kade to know about sleep overs yet, but I could really get used to having you in my bed at night."

"It's because I'm like a human heater, isn't it?"

I could feel her grin against my body. "Yeah, I bet that's it," she insisted as I squeezed her body tighter to mine for a minute in a side hug that squished her tits all up on my body leaving me wanting more of her once again.

15. DADDY IS BACK

WE HAD THAT NIGHT TOGETHER AFTER FINDING OUT KAYLA WASN'T pregnant and then duty called for both rescue and the club. I spent the next two days on with rescue and now I was knee deep in the middle of a run for the club. Smoke had explained that our particular chapter of Aces High didn't dabble a whole lot in the illegal shit, but this was second run where we had a van full of guns headed south to the guys from the Tallahassee Chapter.

"This going to be a regular thing?" I had asked him before we took off. I was a full member this time, so I felt I had the right to ask those questions.

He shook his head. "Nope. Shouldn't have fallen on us this time either, but with the Hounds fucking around with the last delivery we all thought this was safer."

"The Tallahassee Chapter ever going to pull out of the illegal shit?"

Smoke blew out a breath. "They got into some shit a while back when their prez was protecting his woman. They went up against a crime family in their area and won, but that win put them in some shit with other organizations. This is about them still paying those dues. Pretty sure this is the last year they'll have their hands dirty. Crusher is over it. He has a few kids with his woman now, and I wouldn't put it past him to hand over the gavel so he can focus on family and the couple of businesses they have established." Smoke chuckled then. "He took all the advice he got from Ghost's daughter a few years back and ran with it. They've turned shit around completely down there now. They used to operate out of a rented space in a strip mall. Crusher had that shit upgraded long ago, but they were so far in the red with that it was bleeding them dry. Now, they're coasting clear and added on quite a bit to the compound they have down there.

"Well, at least they're one step closer to not having to deal with this shit. It would be a damn shame if he got them this far only to get busted with a shipment this size."

"No kidding. That's part of the push with him getting the other businesses up and running. He was sick of the risk involved. When you have a family to think about it changes perspectives."

We drove on for a bit when my cell beeped letting me know I had a message. I saw the voicemail was from Ghost and didn't bother listening to it. Instead, I dialed him right back. "Hey man, I guess we went through a dead zone when you tried to call, what's up?"

"How close are you to the meet?"

I glanced over at Smoke and then to the GPS we had set up. "Looks like we'll be there in under 15 minutes."

"As soon as you make the exchange, I need you to haul ass back here. We have everything under control, but your woman needs you."

"What the fuck? What's going on?"

"Keep your head on the task at hand and know that she's safe. Gillian and her boy are here with us at the clubhouse, locked down until you get back."

"Locked down? What the fuck for?"

Ghost huffed into the phone. "Looks like her ex ransacked her home."

"Where the fuck was the prospect that was supposed to be watching?"

"Distracted," Ghost grumbled, and I could hear the dissatisfaction in his voice as he did. "He's being dealt with. They're here, safe, and waiting on you to get back. Handle your shit, tell Smoke to get you both back in one piece and quick-like."

"Yeah, thanks for taking care of them," I told him and received a grunt in response before the line disconnected.

"What's going down?"

I relayed the information to Smoke who simply shook his head. "Sometimes this shit is absolutely fucked. What that asshole was thinking, I will never know. His club ain't gonna like the spotlight he's putting on them with this shit."

"Doesn't look like he gives two fucks about that spotlight so long as he gets what he thinks he wants."

Smoke glanced over at me, a puzzled look on his face. "Explain," he ordered.

"Come on, it's one of those cases where he lost the thing he chose. He lost the woman he left them for. Now, he suddenly looks back and sees what he thinks he was missing out on. The thing with these guys is there was something lacking there to send him to someone else to begin with."

"You saying your own woman wasn't worthy of him?"

"Nope. I'm saying he's never been worthy of her and feels that at a soul-deep level maybe he doesn't understand. It's what led to his dissatisfaction to begin with. On some level we can all sense if something is off in a relationship. We either stick it out because we're stubborn or too lazy to look for something better or we get in touch with that feeling and do something about it. In his case, he cheated and then walked away." I shrugged my shoulders.

"That's some deep shit."

"It's the truth. Most people just don't want to acknowledge why things feel off, especially if they're feeling more than the other person seems to be. I think that's why some people cheat. They're proactively hurting the person that they think will eventually hurt them by not returning their affection to the extent they want. Either that or they're not feeling it and just too cowardly to walk away first."

"Shit, maybe you should start offering couples counseling and shit. Sounds like you have that shit on lock down."

I laughed. "I took some Psychology in college, but everything I just spouted off about, I learned from observation and living life." We both sat quietly for a bit as Smoke guided us to where we were meeting the guys from the Tallahassee Chapter.

"She'll be just fine," Smoke finally chimed in.

"I know. It just pisses me off that this shit went down while I was away."

"Most likely went down because you were away. Bet anything that asshole's been watching and waiting for a time when you weren't around."

"Strange then that we haven't had any Hound trouble on this run."

"I'm thinking he didn't clue in his club to his activities, though they would have probably taken his actions a little better if he had. At least then they might have waylaid us, got the shipment, maybe a couple Aces members to take in retaliation for the two we nabbed last time and those that were left dead."

I nodded, though I wasn't certain Smoke caught the gesture. He was right. Joe seemed to be operating on his own agenda outside of his club's reach. I wasn't sure if that was for the best or if it would end up making the situation worse in the end. Either way, I knew I was over this run and wanted to get back home to my woman. She had to be going crazy with all this happening.

We were pulling in beside a cargo van before I knew it and plates were swapped from one vehicle to the other before the guys grabbed the keys to the box van we'd been driving. "This is the last one," the one whose kutte labeled him as Tricky managed to say with a grunt as he dropped the keys into Smoke's palm.

"Thank fuck too. My woman's about to pop any day. Last thing I need is to be away when that happens. She'd never forgive me. Hell, she'd hunt me down and kill my ass if I got hauled to the big house for this shit before I get to meet our son," the other man chimed in. He turned to me then and smiled before offering his hand. "Don't believe we've had the pleasure, man. I'm Court."

I shook my head and laughed as I told him my road name. "Surfer," I managed to get out on a chuckle.

"Our newbie is still a bit embarrassed by his name," Smoke informed them.

Court and Tricky both laughed. "You'll get used to it soon enough. Suits you though. At least you have the look and you weren't some Bubba, cornbread fucker who never saw the ocean a day in his life."

"Yeah, dude, guess it could be worse."

"Fuck man, you can't be embarrassed about the name if you go around saying shit like that. You call everyone 'brah' and 'broski' too?"

"Fuckin' hell, I can't get away from it. Been calling everyone and everything with a pulse dude for so long, it's just second nature."

"Surfer," he started to say something, but the trill of my phone's ringtone interrupted. I glanced down and saw it was Gillian.

"Sorry, I have to take this. Some asshole broke into my woman's place earlier." It was all the explanation I was giving before I walked away and answered the phone.

"Gillian, are you okay?"

"That fucker tossed my fucking house, Gray! He broke shit. Important shit that I can't replace, and it's just... it's just... FUCK!" She yelled at the end.

"Baby, where's Kade?"

"Leanne has him right now. She thought I could use a

minute to blow off some steam. I know you're on club business right now, but I really needed to hear your voice."

"Any time, baby. We're about to wrap things up here. I'll be headed back soon. I'm coming straight to you, baby."

"Please, hurry." The desperation in her voice was a kick to the gut and all I wanted was to be there so that I could hold her and make it better. My own personal vengeance would have to wait until my woman was settled again.

"Be there soon, G."

I hung up and moved back over to where Smoke was still standing with Court and Tricky. "Sorry to hear about your troubles man. That's rough this prick trying to come back into their lives and cause trouble like that," Tricky mentioned.

"Dude, I'm about to teach that asshole a lesson that he's still learning from ten years down the road."

Court laughed. "I think you mean a lesson he's still recovering from."

"That too," I admitted. "My woman is one of the good ones. Her kid is the shit. That asshole doesn't deserve to breathe their air let alone cause them this kind of stress."

"Let us know if you need anything. We can make sure he disappears from your area." I nodded and then turned to head to the cargo van we would be riding back in.

"Thanks. We really have to go so I can get back and see to this shit. Good luck with the impending birth, man."

"Thanks," Court called out and then Smoke was behind the wheel making his adjustments before we were on our way back home.

BEFORE WE GOT out of the van Smoke turned to me and stilled my movements by placing his hand on my shoulder. "I know I'm new to the parenting game, but I was an uncle for a while before," he started to say before his sister and brother-in-law – our club brother - were killed. I watched him choke back that emotion instead and physically shake it off. "I was an uncle to a little boy before, and now he's my responsibility full time. If you need anything, someone to talk to, someone to watch Kade for you guys while you deal with this shit, you just say the word."

"I think you and Poppy both have enough on your shoulders, but I appreciate the offer."

Smoke nodded his head to me and then let go of my arm so I could go check on Gillian.

"Thank God you're back," Gillian whispered into my ear. She was in my arms not two minutes after I pushed through the doors of the clubhouse.

"Good to feel you wrapped around me like this, baby. How are you holding up? How's Kade?"

She grinned up at me then. "What is this the inquisition? I'm fine, just frustrated. I don't like being hidden away from my life. It sends that asshole the wrong message that he can fuck with me and my life will be disrupted. I don't like it."

"I know, babe, but I'd rather be safe than sorry right now, especially since Kade is part of his focus and he doesn't know what's going on there."

"I thought about telling him today, but I couldn't figure

out a good damn way to tell my son that his father is a piece of shit who gave him away for some pussy that didn't even last that long considering the price he paid for it." She huffed out a frustrated sigh. "I thought I'd be able to tell him and be honest without it hurting him when he's older, but I'm not sure I'll get the option to wait now."

I took Gillian by the hand as soon as I was able to pull her arms from around me and guided us over to a quiet corner. There weren't that many people hanging around the club-house tonight and I was thankful for it. The last thing we needed to see while having a serious discussion was one of my brothers getting his dick sucked.

"I know you wanted to wait to minimize the damage you think it will do for him to hear how much of a dick his father is, but I don't think it will get any easier with time. It might be easier for him to hear now. Hasn't he asked any questions about his dad?"

"When he started school and other kids had their fathers pick them up for school he started asking, but I didn't really have to tackle that because his grandmother was the one who answered him."

"What the hell?"

"I used to let him get off the bus at her house. The day he asked that, and she told him she could arrange for him to meet his daddy I started taking him to Beth's house. After a couple weeks she promised to never bring Joe up around him again until I had that conversation with Kade first."

"That's fucked. What did Kade say about it?"

She laughed. "He asked her if his dad knew about him, and when she told him that of course he did Kade got angry.

He told her then he didn't want to meet him because he should have already been there if he really wanted to be."

"Smart beyond his years," I commented. She hummed her agreement. "Smart enough to understand that much on his own then he's ready to hear the truth from his mom. I bet he already overheard some things at some point and that's why he responded to her that way."

She shrugged her shoulders a minuscule amount. "Maybe."

"Tell me what happened today," I prompted her.

"I got home from work with Kade, and I didn't even realize that the lock on the door wasn't engaged. I just went through the motions of getting us into the house like I normally would. Only, once we pushed through the door Kade screamed out, "Mom!" and I glanced up to see that everything was simply wrecked. My couch was sliced open, artwork on the wall was busted to pieces or shredded. Even the goddamn carpet was ripped up in spots. I don't know what the hell to do about that. The house isn't mine. It's a rental. I'm going to lose my deposit and be charged for fixing everything that's fucked up. There were parts of the wall that looked like a sledgehammer had been taken to it and then there was the message on the wall."

"What message?" I asked as the hair on the back of neck stood on end.

She glanced up at me guiltily. "Spread for the Aces and I'll take what's mine."

"What the fuck?" I growled and launched up off the sofa scanning the room looking for Ghost. I found him sitting at the bar watching us. He was apparently waiting for this reaction because he started marching in my direction the minute he saw it. "You said they were fine; you never mentioned a threat scrawled on her walls!"

He held up his hands to me in the universal gesture of surrender. "They were fine. We had them taken care of. The guys waited around for the cops to show to inventory the damage for Gillian's insurance claim and for her landlord. They were here earlier too asking her questions about who she thought could be behind it. Kade and Gillian have been safe with us, brother. They're fine."

"I can see they're fine, but I should have been told."

"What would you have done? You were already nearly to the meet when I called you to let you know, that meant you were going to be headed right back once you dropped off the shit the Tallahassee guys needed." His eyes darted quickly to Gillian to see if she was following along. She was, but she didn't seem overly curious to know what I had been dropping off, which was a good thing. "You're back now. Shit's handled. You can figure out your next move from here on. This is what the brotherhood is about. We help out when you can't be here, and you trust us to do so." He tipped his chin at me, and I nodded in agreement.

"Sorry, it was just a shock."

"I know it was, Surfer. Kind of glad you weren't around earlier. Didn't need you running off halfcocked had you witnessed that shit firsthand without the buffer of time and space to have you seeing clearly. We will get this shit nipped in the bud and dealt with, but we're doing it the right way. The way that nothing bad can come back to bite us in the ass later on down the road. You feel me?"

"Yeah, dude. I feel you." He chuckled at my response and then rapped his knuckles on the wooden table just to his left a couple times before turning his attention to Gillian.

"You need anything at all for you or your boy, you just ask." Gillian didn't respond other than to offer up a tight smile to the man. Once he walked away, I took my seat again, only this time I snatched her ass up and tossed her on my lap.

"He meant that. It wasn't an empty offer," I informed her.

"I know. How could I not? I've seen what the club has done for Beth and Abby since her accident. I get that everyone here would bend over backwards to help us out. Knowing that doesn't take away my anger or feeling help-less, or completely fucking pissed that I was pulled from my home today and not allowed to go back." The last word led right into a growl of frustration as she took a moment to blow a stray strand of hair from her eyes. "I just want to kick him in the junk, repeatedly, for every hour I'm displaced because of his childish rampage I want five minutes to go town on his balls with my foot. No, with a baseball bat, because not even my foot wants to touch any part of him."

I let her ramble and rant, chuckling and wincing at the imagery all at once. "Pretty sure he'd be out cold before the first five minutes were up, baby, but I promise to let you get your licks in if we manage to get to a place where that can happen."

"Thanks for that," she told me as she snuggled in closer, dipping her head to the crook of neck where my shoulder started. I could feel her breath there as she snuggled in. Warm little pockets of air billowed out from her to send a shivering tingle through my upper body. She noticed and leaned in to place a kiss on that sensitive spot. Then she flicked her tongue out and licked the spot before breathing on it intentionally.

"Where's Kade?"

"Leanne took him home with her so he wouldn't have to spend the night here."

I moved her back from me then and looked her in the eyes. "You don't want him around here?"

She laughed. "That's not the problem. With the way the guys swooped in today to rescue us, and then Hold 'Em let Kade ride on his motorcycle with him, I was afraid the guys would find us a new place to stay. Kade was so excited about all the guys that he forgot why they were even there."

That made me feel marginally better about the day. The kid definitely had an early fascination with bikes and bikers. It wouldn't surprise me if he ended up patching in down the road. I hate to think he got that shit from his dad, since from what Gillian mentioned before he hadn't been all that into the biker lifestyle when they were together. Instead, I chose to believe that Kade was fascinated with the lifestyle thanks to the introduction to our world that he got from me.

"We need to talk about how long you two are going to be around. I want you both on lockdown until we locate Joe."

"What? What does that even mean?"

"It means you will both be here and if you have to leave you do so with an escort."

"We can't live like that, Gray. Kade has school and I have work. That's not possible."

"We'll make it a soft lockdown for now, baby, but it has

to happen. Someone will be there to drop you off and pick you up. Same for Kade. We'll let you know so you can make sure whoever has to pick him up has permission with the school."

"I don't like this, and honestly I don't think it's one bit necessary."

"Do you remember what your house looks like?"

She grumbled something under her breath before glancing back up at me. "I don't want to feel like a prisoner because that asshole can't control himself. It's not fair."

"Life ain't fair, sweetheart. I know you have to be teaching that shit to Kade. Listen, I get where you're coming from. See my point of view on this too though. I don't know what the hell I would have done if that call from Ghost today had been worse than it was. If he had been there, hurt you, took Kade, or any combination of those things. Jesus. I honestly wouldn't have been able to get over the fact that I had failed at protecting you. So, don't think of it as him screwing with your life. Think of it as you giving me a little peace of mind until we figure this shit out, okay?"

"Fine, but we're still going to work and school. That's non-negotiable."

I didn't like it, even though I understood her reasoning and the fact that life went on around us despite the drama we had going on. "Okay, we'll try it that way first. If there's any sign of trouble though, we're renegotiating terms."

She grinned then. "Renegotiating or you're just going to tell me that I have to do what you say and keep us on lock-down anyway?"

"Well, I'll throw in some awesome massages and other things to keep you happy while you have to be stuck here."

"Hmm, I might rethink my earlier stance. Let's renegotiate now!"

I laughed and then stood up, depositing her feet on the floor in front of me. Then I took her hand and we walked down the back hallway to the room they had put Gillian in for the day. Since I had been staying at Smoke's apartment, I hadn't needed my own room at the clubhouse. It looked like I was finally going to make use of one of them for more than to sleep off the incredible drunk after I officially became a member.

THE NEXT MORNING, we came out to the main room and saw that there was a breakfast buffet set up on the bar. It wasn't that unusual from what I'd been told, but also not a common occurrence. It was normally something the women put together whenever the club had out of town visitors staying on the premises.

"We have guests in?" I asked and Tuck glanced over at me.

"Nah Surfer, we're all in for a meeting this morning. Leanna and Poppy stopped in to put something together for us."

"I didn't realize," I started to say when I heard my cell beep from my pocket."

Tuck laughed. "That's probably your notice there, dude."

"Not you too," I groaned.

He just laughed and walked off while draining some the fresh cup of coffee he'd just poured himself.

"You know if it didn't look like it bothered you, they probably wouldn't keep tormenting you like that."

"I know," I admitted. "They like doing it so I play their little game."

"You clever dog, you."

I shrugged my shoulders and turned to take in the room. I was wondering where Kade was since Leanne was here this morning getting breakfast ready for the men. "He's in the bathroom," she told me as she slid in beside us and handed Gillian and me each a plate.

"You a mind reader now?"

"Nope, I just saw you looking around and figured since that's what I would be looking for..."

I leaned in and gave her a quick side hug. "Thanks for seeing to him last night."

"Get your hands off my woman!" Ghost called out from across the room. "Gillian, put your man on a leash!" He ordered to everyone else's amusement.

"Ghost, you know I'm only yours!"

"Damn right, woman because no one could throw it to you as good as I do!"

"Throw what?" Kade asked innocently as he stepped out of the bathroom for the last bit of conversation being yelled across the room. "You play ball, Ms. Leanne?"

"Sure do, honey!" She answered back while everyone else in the room simply laughed.

"What's so funny about that?" Kade asked them as his face screwed up in anger. "Girls can play too, you know."

"That's my boy! You get 'em!" Gillian encouraged her son.

"You good out here getting him breakfast and ready while I go see what's up?"

"Yeah, my car is here anyway. Once we're good to go we can just head out."

"No. I thought we got this straightened out last night? It's not safe right now."

"Come on! Joe might be an asshole and show his shit by destroying my things, but he would never physically hurt one of us."

"You don't know him anymore. Did you ever think he'd have it in him to abandon his own kid?" she didn't answer so carried on. "Did you ever see him breaking into your home? Destroying the shit you worked hard to get? Did you picture him turning your life upside down for his own amusement?"

She huffed at me, then growled before making sure she wouldn't be overheard by Kade. "I get it. We'll wait until you're done. I won't have him late to school though, so be wary of the time."

The door shut on the room where we held church and each man who hadn't already done so took his seat around the table. "I contacted Tonka last night after we found Gillian's house trashed."

"What did that ugly fucker have to say?" Hopper asked.

"He said that one of our bitches having her home vandalized wasn't any of his concern." I was on the edge of my seat when Ghost held up his hand. "I explained to him that if his men were going to start targeting innocent women and children associated with our club then we would consider it free reign to do the same to them."

"What the fuck?" Wren called out.

"Not that we'd ever do that," Ghost clarified. "He doesn't need to know that though."

Smoke's cell started going on. After glancing down at it he moved away from the table and took the call. "Aren't you supposed to be here already?"

He hit speakerphone and everyone got quiet. "Just picked my fuckin bike up and scraped myself off the side of the road. Some fuckers in a blue Ford pickup truck, older model ran me off the road when I was escorting Beth and Abby there. Beth ain't here. I guess I got knocked out for a bit. Couldn't have been too long, but..." his voice cut out as the phone crackled with static. "Put Bluetooth on through the helmet. Going to look for her."

"Hold up, didn't you just say you got your bell rung hard enough to knock you the fuck out? You sit tight, we're sending someone to your location," Ghost ordered.

"I think I see her," we heard Hold 'Em announce. Then there was nothing beyond the roar of his engine until we all heard that sound die away too. "Beth!" His voice yelling. "Shit, Beth! Is Abby okay?"

"S-s-she's fine," we could faintly make out Beth's stuttering voice. "They were ramming my car!" The stutter was replaced by a frantic shrill tone. I saw Joe in the passenger side. What the hell is Gillian's ex-boyfriend doing trying to run me off the side of the road?"

"Let's worry about that later, okay. It's part of the reason we were headed to the clubhouse. I need to look at that," he told her. I was pretty sure he had forgotten that we were all still listening in through the Bluetooth on his helmet.

"I just bumped my head. It's okay."

"No, the fuck you aren't. Your lip is bleeding and fuck me if you aren't going to have a shiner by tomorrow." There was something in his voice, emotion that got caught up. We all heard it, and every single one of us glanced around the table to see if we were the only ones. Damn. I hadn't been able to have that talk with Hold 'Em that I had wanted because of everything else going on.

"Holden?" The question in her voice didn't sound like it was about what was happening with Joe. Damn. I hoped that he did right by her. The woman had too much bad luck in her life already.

"He better not fuck her over," Tuck called out.

"Shit!" We all heard Hold 'Em call out and then the line went dead.

I stood immediately, because I knew time was running short anyway. There was no need to wait for permission to leave, I was sure that my brothers would understand what I was going to do. As it turned out, I had not one single moment to spare. "Gillian!" I called out just as she opened the clubhouse door with Kade in tow.

She turned and glared at me. "Sorry, Gray. I told you we were not going to be late."

"You're not going at all!" I wasn't proud of the fact that I shouted it at her from across the room, but I needed to get her attention. She wasn't seeing this for what it was. They were both in danger.

She didn't even answer me. Instead, she huffed and then proceeded to head out of the door, tugging Kade along behind her. He was obviously reluctant and turned around watching me as they went. It took no time at all for me to cross the room and catch up to them before they could make it two steps beyond the door.

"Gillian, this isn't a game. You are both staying here today."

"I will not deal with this type of shit, Gray. Not even from you. We have lives to live," she started to say before I cut her off.

"And I'm trying to make sure you're both alive to live them. Your ex just ran Beth off the road," I shouted in her face, forgetting for a moment that Kade was standing right there.

"What?"

"Is that going to be enough to finally get through to you that this is dangerous? Does someone have to die to get it through to you?"

"Jesus! Kade, go back inside!"

"Is Ms. Beth okay?"

"She's going to be fine, buddy. Sorry, I'm just really upset that someone tried to hurt her."

"Was it the person who wrecked our house?" The kid asked.

I nodded my head.

"You gonna beat his ass?"

"Kade!" Gillian yelped out, exasperated. The boy didn't take his eyes from me.

"I am going to make sure he doesn't mess with you, your mom, or Beth ever again."

"Promise?"

"You got it, little dude."

He turned then to his mom. "Sorry mom." Before she could respond he went back inside the clubhouse to wait for us.

"Was she hurt?"

"She's shaken up. From what we could hear she has a busted lip and black eye. Not sure if there was anything else since the line went dead."

"Is someone going to get her?"

"Hold 'Em is with her," I let her know.

"Where was he when she was run off the road then?"

"He was knocked out on the side of the road after having been their first victim today."

Her hand flew up to cover her mouth in a lame attempt to hold her gasp in. "What in the world is happening? How is Joe behind all of this? I just don't understand. He was never a violent person. He was just careless with people's hearts."

"Well, baby, he ain't the same person you used to know. A lot has happened in his life, including some cunt fuckin' him over after he gave up his son for her. I'm thinking that puts women pretty far down on his list of people he'll give a fuck about from here on out."

"That's just crazy," she whispered.

"Well, so is giving up your son for a woman. I'm thinking

his kind of crazy has just been escalating for years and you have been blissfully unaware of the favor he did the both of you when he walked away all those years ago."

Before anything more could be said the rumble of a bike caught my attention and I looked up just in time to watch Beth pull her car in followed closely by Hold 'Em who didn't appear to be sitting too steady on his ride.

"Fuck!" I hissed out as I started moving toward him. "Get Smoke. Tell him to get the first aid bag ready. Interrupt their damn meeting if they're still in there," I ordered her before catching Hold 'Em when he tipped over while trying to dismount the bike.

"Shit," he slurred.

"Oh my God! Is he okay?" Beth shouted as she ran from her car.

"He'll be okay. He took a tumble before he caught up to you, and he should not have been riding." I held on to him and shuffled slowly toward the door. Hold 'Em was a solid guy built of muscle from all the working out he did. It's not a stretch to say I was straining a bit while trying to hold his ass up and move him forward at the same time when he looked all but ready to pass the fuck out on me. "Get Abby inside and yell for someone to come help me with this monster-sized fucker." He wasn't exceedingly tall. He was a match to my six, one height. His bulk was another thing entirely. The bastard had been working off a lot of steam and taking it out on the weights lately. I hadn't really paid much attention to exactly how ripped he was getting until this moment though.

"All right, come on," Wren hissed out as he took some of

Hold 'Em's weight off my hands. "Jesus, how much working out has he been doing lately?"

I laughed. Then I was grunting again as we managed to get the guy inside the clubhouse. "We might need to get his ass to the hospital. There's no equipment here that can check to make sure he doesn't have a bleed or dangerous swelling in that giant head of his."

"Already called a bus. They're on the way," Smoke told me as he moved in. "Have you done any preliminary checks?"

"Fuck no, caught the bastard in the parking lot before he went down, and struggled just to get his ass in here."

"Beth, do you remember where you were when he went down?"

"No. I didn't even realize he wasn't following me anymore until that truck ran into me."

"Okay, do you know where you were when that first happened?"

"I had just taken a right off of Pritchard St. onto Cedar."

"Check Pritchard just before it intersects with Cedar. See if any cameras caught anything," Smoke said into his phone.

I nodded, knowing he had one of the cops in town checking security footage.

"Is he going to be okay?"

"We're going to get him taken care of," Smoke assured her.

"Let's get you cleaned up and checked out while we wait, okay, darlin'?" I asked her and then pulled her off to the side, taking the first aid kit with me as I went.

"I want to go with him," Beth demanded before she turned and started searching the room with her eyes. When they finally landed on Gillian, she heaved a sigh of relief. "Can you keep Abby so I can go make sure he's going to be okay?"

"Yeah, you know I will," Gillian offered, though I could see in her eyes that she was swimming in guilt. "I'm so sorry, Beth!" Her voice broke on Beth's name and she sank down into a chair, shoulders shaking. I wanted to go to her, but I needed to see to Beth's wounds first and make sure it wasn't anything more than the superficial cuts and bruising I could see with my eyes.

"Gillian, what that asshole did isn't your fault. It's not like you even attempted to invite him back into your life," I reminded her as I worked on Beth.

"Still, this is all because of..."

"It's because we're rival clubs, baby. Nothing else. Stop thinking like that. This shit is not on you."

"He's right," Beth agreed. "Joe did these things. You couldn't have anticipated this or stopped him, honey. Don't even try to take the brunt of his issues on your own shoulders."

"Who are we scooping?" A voice called out from the door. I glanced up to see Dave Holland, one the paramedics that worked the opposite shifts to my own.

"Hey Dave," I tipped my chin to Hold 'Em, who we had laid out on a table. "He got bumped off his bike earlier. Climbed back on to go find this one, because the same truck that took him out was attempting to push her off the road too. He got her all the way here, and then he collapsed as he tried to get off his bike. When he dumped the bike, it knocked him out for a bit, not sure how long. Couldn't have been too long though we found her just around the corner from where he think he went down."

"Shit, why didn't he call for a pickup? Jesus, I can't believe he was able to ride if he was that rattled."

"I'm guessing adrenaline did him no favors, but also managed to get his ass here."

"All right, we're out of here," Dave called out as they lifted the gurney, they'd moved Hold 'Em to.

"Beth here wants to go with him," I told them.

"She family?"

"His fiancée," I informed them. Beth looked ready to protest so I kicked her shin to shut her up. She chirped out a quick 'ouch,' but played it off as she touched her lip. "Besides, she can probably do with a better lookin' over too. They knocked her off the road, and she hit her head when the car came to a stop."

"Ok, sweetheart, come on and load up. Stay out of the way though."

"Sure." Beth loaded up with Hold 'Em and the ambulance crew and they were gone within minutes of their arrival.

I went straight to Gillian and pulled her in my arms. "Call work, and take some emergency leave, baby. No more fighting me on this. That could have been you and Kade this morning, and if you'd left before I came out there wouldn't have been anyone trailing you two to help you out when you got run off the road."

I felt her body shaking again as she sobbed into my chest. "I'm so sorry. I honestly didn't think," she managed to get out. I rubbed little circles on her back while she pulled herself together. "I'm sorry," she whispered into my chest once more.

"It's okay, baby. I'm going to get it taken care of. No more worries, I promise."

Little did I know I wouldn't be able to keep that promise just yet.

16. SENDING A MESSAGE

THERE COMES A TIME WHEN EVERYTHING THAT YOU MAY HAVE wondered about suddenly becomes clear. It had been months since I was given my position with the club, which also meant we'd been housing two prisoners that entire time. The two Hounds we kept as leverage were still in our care. I had asked before why we were keeping them, feeding the bastards, and making sure they had plush lodgings. Granted, they were unable to leave those lodgings, but let it not be said we treated the men very well while they were in our care outside of the beatdown they both got periodically when we questioned them about the operations of their club. To be sure, the Hounds had to think their men were dead by now. They were about to get the surprise of a lifetime.

We bound the man we were sending back and tied a note to him, but the bastard was literally crying about having to leave his prison.

"Please, look, I'll do whatever you want, make sure they get their message, but don't send me back there. If I show up looking like I've been treated well they're going to assume I earned that treatment by telling y'all shit."

"Thought you didn't know anything to tell us?" Wren asked him since that was always his mantra when he got the periodic beatdowns.

"I fuckin' don't, but they ain't the smartest bunch of assholes on the planet, you know?"

"We fuckin' know considering you're delivering this message because they're fucking with our women and children."

"What the fuck?" The man was truly taken aback to learn his club had gone after our women, or maybe it was the kids that got his attention, either way he was legitimately shocked about it.

"You didn't know the bastards you aligned yourself with would stoop that low?" I asked the question, and he just stood there shaking his head back and forth.

"Women are almost always off limits, but kids, man. No way. No way Tonka is behind letting them fuck with kids."

"What do you think Tonka is going to do to you when he sees you looking well fed and groomed with nary a bruise on your body?"

"Fuck!" The man hissed out through his teeth. "I'm dead. 'Preciate the cozy comfort you boys kept me in though. Fucking death row inmates wish they were your prisoners. I fuckin' got mixed in with the wrong crew. No lie about that."

We could see the regret swimming in his eyes as he spoke. I wasn't sure if I felt bad for him though considering this asshole was one of the men who had tried to end my life on the side of a road not too many months ago in order to steal the shipment of guns and ammo I happened to be driving around.

There was a small part of me that hoped that his own club would just be happy to have him back in one piece and hopeful that they could get their other man back too. The rest of me didn't give a shit what happened to him so long as his club left my woman and her kid the fuck alone.

It took us twenty minutes of circling their laughable compound before we finally got a clear moment to dump the dude out of the van. That's exactly what we did too. Wren opened the slider door and I put a boot in his ass. We had only slowed down just enough that he wouldn't get too banged up, but enough that he was going to feel that fall for a little bit if his own club brothers didn't end him first. It was a compromise the men and I made in order to try to make him look at least a little banged up. What can I say? I had a bit of a heart. Besides, we wanted to see how well our message would be received.

It didn't take long to find out. Later that evening we got the call that Daisy's Diner had been hit. Daisy took some damage too when a shattered window spewed glass all over while she attempted to shelter a customer. A message had been left behind at the scene. "Spread for the Aces, get dealt the same damage."

I glanced over at Smoke who was preoccupied with something on his phone as we glanced around the parking lot and then inside the diner looking for anything else that might be useful. Thankfully, the guys already had the place wired with video so we were going to be able to see firsthand who had done the damage.

"Something doesn't feel right about this," I muttered as I glanced around at the damage. A few of the windows had been busted out and then there was the message sent through one of them taped to a brick.

"You're right," Ghost chimed in. "It feels too juvenile. I can't see Tonka condoning this shit in his club's name. I'm going to force a sit down."

Mick was standing just off to the side. "Daisy gonna be okay?" I asked him.

"She'll be fine. Just a few superficial cuts to deal with. She was more concerned with her clientele not wanting to come back in to eat once we get this shit cleaned up. Daisy was Mick's old lady, and Mick was our security officer in charge of all the techie stuff which is why the diner had one of the best video surveillance systems out there. "I pulled the video, and have it downloaded to my laptop. We can comb through it back at the clubhouse. Too many eyes roaming around here."

"I have to go take care of something. Is everything handled here for now?" Smoke asked of Ghost after he finally pulled himself away from whatever he'd been caught up in on his phone.

"You good?" Ghost asked. Smoke nodded then Ghost signaled he was good to leave. "Chief!"

"What's up boss man?"

"Stop calling me boss man!" Ghost chided him. "Tail him and see what's got his panties in a twist. Maybe it is just your sister or something, but I have a feeling it has more to do with Sophie and Bender."

"On it," Chief told him and then took off for his bike.

"You think he found something on whoever took them out?"

"I know he found out it was no accident. I'm not sure if he's been able to track them down yet or not, but it's looking like it. We do not need to be fighting a war on two fronts right now."

"I'm guessing he knows that and is trying to keep things to himself."

"That's the kind of thinking that gets good men killed," Ghost countered flatly before he sauntered away.

I couldn't really argue with his logic anyway. My part here was done. I had only been asked to come along in case anyone needed extra medical attention. There were already medics from the station there working on the couple people who had a few cuts, and my skills weren't necessary so I hopped back on my bike and got ready to make my way back to the clubhouse when Mick came rushing out of a van in the parking lot.

"Hold on, brother!" He yelled out for me, holding up his hand in a gesture that said he needed a minute before I could head out. He came back out with Ghost, Wren, and Tuck following behind.

Ghost came straight for me. "Need you with Wren and Tuck for a bit. Mick has a clear image of two of the three assholes who were here. Bet your ass the third, the one we couldn't make out, was Joe since the same basic message was passed along here as at your woman's house."

"Are we going after them?"

Ghost nodded his head. "Stay sharp. This looked juvenile

at first glance to me, but it could be a tactic to get us moving on them and straight into an ambush."

"Got it," I answered and then waited for Wren and Tuck to mount up. I turned to Mick then. "You coming with?"

"Nah, gonna go see to Daisy. She may try to pull the tough card, but I can see she's a shaken. I'm needed for that reason more than I need to get the revenge myself. Make those bastards pay, Surfer."

"Bet your ass, dude!" His chin tipped up before he walked away to take care of his woman. As much as I wanted to go check in with my own, I knew I had to get this taken care of. Everything felt like it was sitting at a simmer and at any moment now I would look away only to have it boil over out of control. I couldn't take the chance that Gillian or Kade would be caught up in that. Hell, I needed to add the rest of the club and all of our family and friends to that list too. We were being targeted. That much was clear. What wasn't clear was why they were going for auxiliary people instead of coming direct for our members. That was part of what was bothering me. In all the time the club had bad blood with the Hounds over territorial disputes with the gun running pipe-line, they had never been so blatant, nor had they ever purposely involved family. It was obvious Joe had recruited help, but I was beginning to wonder if he actually had the backing of his club or if he had gone rogue.

WE FOUND two of the assholes at a hole in the wall bar four blocks from the diner. A good Samaritan called in a tip about some idiots talking about trashing a local diner, and we headed there while our eyes on sight kept us up to date about the men's movements. Just before we showed up, I received a text letting us know that one of the men had stepped out the back. It just so happened we pulled right into the back to see the asshole in question getting blown just outside the bar door and beside the dumpster that was set up there. Needless to say, he did not get his happy ending. We handed the woman fifty bucks and told her to get lost. She did so, gladly. It wasn't until I saw the guy's Johnson still hanging out that I realized why she'd been so keen on getting out of there. You could barely see his dick for the forest of hair he had down there.

"Jesus! It looks like you're smuggling a whole 70s disco worth of afro down there," Wren commented with a straight face. Not sure how he managed either. Tuck grinned, but then tapped me on the shoulder and tipped his head toward the door.

"Gonna go make sure his friend shows up for the festivities. Be right back."

I gave him a nod, wondering if it was smart to split up at all, but Wren grinned over at me and indicated I should join him. "I don't know man; I feel kind of bad about putting this guy through any more than he has to carry around on his soul every day." Wren turned to me. "Imagine if you had to go around with the weight of having that tiny little dick get lost in all that..." he swished his hand around in front of him.

"Fuck you!" The man yelled out.

"Fuck me? Not very likely. Even if I swung that way, it would be like tickle torture on my ass and I'd be screaming uncle long before you managed to get close enough to even think about poking my brown eye with that little baby pickle you have."

The man's face turned a bright shade of red, and I could see him twitching and wanting to close his pants up, but every time he flinched like he was going to put his tiny dick away Wren aimed his Barretta down at the man's junk.

"What the fuck do you pussies want?" he finally grew enough balls to shout at us just as Tuck came outside hauling another Hound. Tuck moved him to stand beside his buddy who glanced down and then back over toward Wren and myself.

"The fuck, man? Put your cock away," he warned.

"Been trying to," the asshole mumbled.

Tuck couldn't hold the laughter in as he tipped his head to the side seemingly to get a better angle on the view. "Seriously, have you never had a woman complain about all that you have going on down there?"

"Fuck off," he cried out again. As fun as this was, I really just wanted to be home with Gillian and Kade, so I figured I'd move this along.

"Who were you with earlier tonight?" I asked.

"You fuckin' saw who I was with before you interrupted my blow job."

"No, dumbass, we saved that woman from the choking hazard you got going on there – and I don't mean that in a complimentary way. I asked who you were with earlier tonight, say about the time you decided to do something completely idiotic like busting up Daisy's Diner."

The man Tuck had just brought out laughed. The one whose dick was still trying to swing free in the wind – if it were long enough to do so – glanced cautiously between Wren and myself. "Pussy ass bitches can't even keep your women safe. You think you deserve to be in their lives if we can get to them so easily?" That, again, was the newcomer to the party.

I watched his smug face a moment before I leaned back and sent a kick straight into his gut. We all watched as he doubled over, sputtering for air, unable to suck any in because I'd just knocked the wind out of him. "You must be stupid, because I remember asking who you were with not why you were there."

He grinned up at me after a coughing spell finally got his breathing sorted. "Fuck you."

"Not my type," I told him before stomping my boot down on the ring, middle, and index fingers of his right hand. Then I ground my shoe back and forth over them for a little extra oomph.

"Fuuuuck!" He screamed.

Wren had moved closer to the other man by now and had his gun aimed at his junk again. "Now, we already know who it was, we're just looking for a little confirmation before we finish up our business with you two."

"We ain't rats," he informed us.

"You know what? I really don't care if you are or aren't. I need to know where to find Joe."

"Don't know," he said before Wren pulled the trigger,

after a swift adjustment in angle. The bullet missed the asshole's manhood but managed to hit him in the toe.

"Holy shit, holy shit! They fucking shot my foot."

"Where is Joe?" I asked once more.

"He ain't here," the second man said as he stupidly got to his feet. The idiot didn't even see the jab I threw as it was coming. Once he was down for the count his cohort started singing like a fucking bird.

"Listen, I don't know where he is now, but the fucker goes to hide out at his momma's house when he thinks he's in trouble. You should check there or at his ex-wife's house. He's been going around there a lot since he got bumped up in the club ranks. She didn't want him when he was just a prospect."

Damn if that didn't sound a little too familiar.

"She's talking to him more now."

"Then why the fuck would he be sniffing around his kid and the kid's mom?" I wasn't about to give him their names even if he may have already learned them from Joe.

The man laughed. "Joe ain't got no kids. His woman would nail his nuts to a door if he did. Shit, that bitch would fuck him up if he dared even speak of ever being with another woman, let alone dared to have a kid with one."

I cocked my head to the side. "What the fuck did you think you were hitting the diner and that woman's house for?"

"He said he had a score to settle with some punk in your club and the only way to do that would be to fuck with the people who couldn't handle their own shit. The women."

"He used you for his own agenda. Wonder what your

prez is going to think knowing you started a war he didn't fuckin' sanction?" The man's eyes widened then he turned his face down to look at his brother lying there out cold on the ground. The douchebag wasn't exactly out cold any longer, he was just playing dead like the cowardly little pussy he was.

I was tired of this. Neither of them was going to have any useful information, at least none that they would give up without us wasting more time. I nodded to Wren who pistol-whipped the idiot. We watched him crumble and land on his buddy. I took out my cell and grabbed a snapshot because the way he fell was comical. His waist was evenly draped over his buddy's head. It was clear by the way his pants were pulled down below his ass that his dick was out. His kutte was proudly displaying that he was a member of the Hounds too. His buddy, still trying to play dead beneath his brother, had to have that massive jungle of pubes hanging all in his face, but he was managing to stay still. Unfortunately for him that meant I got the picture of the year.

I sent it to Ghost.

> Surfer: Some leverage when you talk to Tonka. Let him know what these pricks get up to when they think no one is looking.

His response was immediate.

> Ghost: lol I don't even want to know how you managed that. Anything good come of it, other than that shot?

Surfer: Just that I am more convinced that this was a rogue operation, and Joe led them to believe the club would be behind it when he recruited help.

Ghost: Well, what do you know. Tonka wants a meet now. Thanks for the pic. He was resistant before.

Surfer: You want us to scoop these assholes up, send 'em to meet their maker, or leave 'em?"

Ghost: Leave them. Tonka's gonna have them scooped up. Part of our good will mission to get him to reel in his rogue. Details when you get back.

I gave the rally sign and we left the assholes lying outside a dive bar that had been named Buddies. Don't know if that was a fuck up on the owner's part, if he meant "Buddy's," or if he really meant it was just a place for buddies. Either way, I laughed at the irony of having these two buddies being found the way they were situated outside of a place with that name. Perfect.

17. TOO QUIET

THE CLUBHOUSE WAS STILL. THERE WAS NO OTHER WAY TO PROPERLY describe it. In the two weeks since we confronted two of the assholes Joe had convinced to help him fuck with our club nothing had happened. No retaliation for the picture we sent of the idiots looking like they were giving each other a decent blow in the alley behind the bar. There had been no more sightings of Joe either. Tonka had promised Ghost that the man was going to be sent on a run that would have him out of town for a few weeks at minimum and then he would be barred from getting anywhere near Gillian or Kade since they were claimed by me.

Normally, I didn't think any club president would get involved in a way to keep a man's kid from him, but in this case, he knew the background and the fact that Kade had never been Joe's beyond the deposit that made him.

"This just doesn't feel right," I mumbled. The only person around to hear me was Tuck and he was busy inventorying the booze behind the bar.

"What's that, Surfer?"

"This, the fuckin' quiet, it doesn't feel right."

Tuck stopped what he was doing and really gave me a sharp once over. "My momma used to always tell me never to look a gift horse in the mouth, but my dad told me that's some shitty advice given the Trojan horse shit." He winked at me. "If your gut is telling you something maybe you should talk it over with Ghost. At the very least, hit up Mick and see if he's noticed anything of concern."

"Yeah, maybe I'll do that," I told him as I removed my ass from the stool where I'd parked it earlier in the day. I didn't have shit going on for another two days. Gillian was back at work and Kade was in school again. Neither of them had any issues so far, but there was no telling how long that would last. I was getting itchy about things, so I decided to go see Ghost about it.

"What can I do for you?" The man asked as I stepped into his office. His unusual teal-color eyes glanced up at me briefly and then shifted quickly back down to the work he was doing on his laptop.

"I don't really know. To be honest, all the quiet is getting to me. Everyone's gone back to normal, but it isn't sitting right with me. I've got that feeling," I started to say and then remembered I didn't need to filter my thoughts because Ghost had served too, and he would understand what I was about to say. "You know that twitch in your gut before you head out on a mission? Everyone keeps saying how it'll be routine, and you'll be back in no time?" he acknowledged my questions only with a slight nod of his head.

"I have this feeling. Shit isn't over and the climax is

waiting just around the corner. I know it's there, but if I warn people the plan might change and then they don't trust that instinct. Do you know what I mean?"

"You think if you tell Gillian you want her to be more careful or stay on lockdown she will balk at the idea because nothing has happened, and they're going back to their routine without incident so far."

"Yeah, basically. I feel this thing though," I repeated as my fist balled up right below where my diaphragm is located. "It's this constant pressure, and the only time I ever feel that is right before shit blows the fuck up. Felt it the night I met Beth. Felt it when I lost my buddy to an IED. I'm not into that bullshit new age stuff, but I swear to you, this feeling is a gift. Blessing or curse depends on what I do with the warning, I guess. I really don't want this to be a fuckin' curse considering who and what is at stake."

"Tell you what," Ghost started to say as he gave me more of his undivided attention. "The asshole has been chomping at the bit for a face-to-face meet. I'll set that up with Tonka. We'll offer to hand over the other man we still have of theirs in trade for his assurance that that dipshit won't be back. At the very least. I'll get his acknowledgement that he will keep Joe on a short leash once he does return."

I nodded. "Yeah, okay," I told him though I still felt that pressure in my gut letting me know nothing had changed. Things were still going to get fucked. It was just a matter of time to see how badly, and who would be affected by the fallout when the dust settled.

OVER THE NEXT two days details were hashed out and we kept a man watching the meeting point. He informed us that they also had a man out there who hadn't spotted him. That was probably for the best since our man had been none other than Mick. He set up some cameras and high-powered microphones so that he could capture everything that happened. To say I wasn't the only one who didn't trust this shit was an understatement.

Mick hadn't been thrilled with the fact that the two goons who had helped Joe out when they trashed the diner had been left alive, let alone without an ass kicking that required hospitalization at the very least. He had been impressed with the pictures we took of them, but it was still very little balm considering his woman had not only been hurt, but was losing business while they cleaned up the diner and got all new windows put in. The windows were something spectacular, an upgrade, and probably made the diner one of the safest places to be in the little town of Cedar Falls. The fuckers were literally bullet-proof works of art. Then again, they were Ninety dollars per square foot and Daisy had damn near floor to ceiling windows lining two sides of her diner. It was a hefty price to pay, but Mick refused to do anything less.

By the time the meet was upon us my whole body seemed to be vibrating with built up tension. So many 'what if' scenarios bounced through my head that I had trouble sorting through all the possibilities. It all fed into my overall anxious appearance, prompting a dress-down from Ghost.

"You are so fuckin' keyed up, I'm rethinking taking you along," he had told me only moments ago.

"It's this feeling churning in my gut," I reminded him. "I know this meet is supposed to be a good thing for us, but the feeling isn't going away. It's getting worse."

Ghost reached back behind the bar and pulled out a bottle of Jack Daniels Black Label. He poured a healthy shot into a tumbler and then slid it my way. "Take the shot, if it helps to calm you before we leave, I won't have a problem with you coming along. I know you have the gut instinct kicking in, and I'm not disregarding that, but Surfer you have to be able to hold it together."

"I love them," I admitted out loud for the first time. It probably shouldn't have been Ghost I was saying it to, but I knew he'd understand. He nodded his head. I took the shot of liquor and he poured another, a bit stronger.

"I get that, and lord knows I've been in your shoes. Hell, lost my woman, and swear to fuck it nearly took me out too. Lost a lot of years with my daughter as a result of how fucked it made me. I get it, better than anyone. I look at Leanne now, and our kids together, and shit... if I were in your shoes, I'd be the same. Doesn't mean someone shouldn't step in and save us from ourselves too before we become the reason our instincts were firing off in the first place."

Fuck my life, but he was right about that. Maybe I was the source of my own troubles. It had been quiet. Things were back to semi-normal except for me feeling off about something I couldn't even put my finger on. I had to put my faith in my club, my brothers, and the fact that they wouldn't purposely let me down.

The second shot went down just as smoothly even though the liquor settled heavily in my stomach at first. Once the slight burn faded though it seemed to take some of my demons on hiatus with it.

"Better?"

"Thanks," I offered in answer.

"Then let's go get this shit taken care of. You have a woman and a kid to get back to."

By THE TIME we got there Tonka's men from the Hell's Hounds were already waiting on us. We knew they were and had planned it that way. They'd been talking freely thinking they were alone, and Mick had picked up their conversation for us to scour over later.

"Ghost," a rotund man with a scraggly, patchwork graying beard called out as we all dismounted our bikes. I assumed this was Tonka, the President of the Hell's Hounds MC. I had never met the man before so I could have been wrong.

"Tonka," Ghost called back confirming my suspicions. He walked over and quickly shook the man's hand before glancing back over his shoulder at us, and then at the cargo van that had pulled in behind us. "I'm not real big on wasting time. Enough of that has gone down."

Tonka laughed heartily. "Well," he called out, quickly

looking over his shoulder to his men. "You heard the man. No need to waste time." Some of the men on the other side of the invisible line we'd drawn between the two clubs laughed. Others didn't. There was some movement toward the back of their ranks and then two of there men started dragging a third out to the forefront. The tossed the beaten and bloodied man at their president's feet.

"I do believe this is the problem we've been having," he stated, and we all glanced down once more. Sure enough, there was tattoo visible on his forearm that had the name Kade in block letters with script around it that read 'lost to regrets'. Well, fuck me. The bastard had a conscious after all. Too bad he went about trying to appease it the wrong fuckin' way.

"As you can see, we've had words about going outside of the club and exacting justice or whatever the fuck he thought he was doing."

"Words aren't going to cut it in this case. He targeted women and children of our club."

"I'm under the impression that the woman and child in question were his," Tonka countered.

"They would have been, but he gave them up years ago," I answered.

Tonka's dark eyes set on me then. "You the new man?"

I tipped my head just enough he could see that I was. "They built a life when he threw them away. She doesn't want to expose her son to the asshole only so he can pull the same stunt again."

"A man tends to learn from the lessons that cause him heartache."

"No one gives a shit about his heartache since he caused it himself." I huffed out a breath and then continued on. "Look, dude, if that asshole truly felt bad and wanted to get his kid back in his life, he would have approached things in an entirely different way. Even the craziest, slowest mother fucker out there would know that breaking in and vandalizing his kid's mother's home – the kid's home – would not be the way to go about doing that."

"You're forgetting that when he tried to do things the right way, you and your club showed up."

"We protect what's ours. Ambushing her at her home when he doesn't even know if the kid knows anything about him wasn't the way to go either. A phone call might have been a good starting point. All that is moot now though, isn't it?"

Tonka glanced down at the body lying at his feet, then he kicked it just hard enough to earn a grunt from the man. Still alive then. "He's learning that he fucked up, again." Tonka then turned his attention back to Ghost. "You have my man here?"

"We do," Ghost confirmed.

"I can't hand this punk over, but I can assure you he's on notice with my club. He steps out of line again we take his patch and his ink the hard way. You won't be having any more trouble."

"Wren," Ghost called, and I turned slightly so I could see the van from my peripheral. He slid the van door open and out walked the second man we'd picked up the day I was shot on the gun run for the club. He swaggered past me and cocked his fingers into a gun emitting a 'pow' noise as he winked at me and continued moving in order to join the ranks of his club brothers.

I didn't think he should have been so cocky about his reentrance into his club since I didn't see the last guy we had sent back amongst their ranks. "Our other man told us you treated them well, better than expected while you had them," Tonka stated as he glared at the cocky son of a bitch who was pounding fists with another member. "Appreciate that considering you had my boy," he admitted.

I glanced at Ghost, but he showed no outward sign of emotion or being caught off guard. I supposed it was a good thing we hadn't just killed them when we first discussed it. "We're good then unless he brings another problem to our doorstep."

Tonka cocked his head to the side. "What exactly are you implying?"

"I'm not implying shit. I'm telling you that if your man, Joe there," he offered up a finger, pointing to the man groaning on the ground, comes after our guy's old lady or kid again and we're going to consider it a very personal attack. Club justice won't suffice any longer. You feel me?"

Tonka nodded. "If he fucks up and you get to him before we do, then we'll call fair game," Tonka conceded. "He has been warned, so any fuck ups are on him."

Ghost nodded his head. "Then we're done here."

"One more thing," Tonka declared halting Ghost in his tracks. "I have it on good authority that your MC won't be running guns through this area any longer."

"We don't run guns, so no clue what you're talking about." Ghost was not about to admit to any criminal activity like that knowing we had the place wired for sound. Not that I thought he'd tip his hat to our rivals as to our activities anyway.

Tonka chuckled. "Just wanted to point out that we won't have any further issues since we don't have the same business plan laid out."

"Good to know," Ghost told him. "I never saw a problem to begin with." On that note, Ghost turned his back on the man. It was a ballsy move but spoke volumes about how secure Ghost was with his men. Tonka was unable to mask his disbelief right away. His jaw dropped and it took a moment to get himself under wraps again.

"Let's load him up and head out, Hounds!" Tonka called out in an overly loud voice. I wasn't sure what his men saw in him that they blindly followed his orders. He wasn't someone I would have lasted long serving under in the military, and certainly wouldn't have commanded my respect or allegiance with the way he conducted business. Having a fellow brother laid out before his enemy – broken and bloody – whether he deserved it or not, wasn't a way to earn fans or loyalty.

"That was anticlimactic. Didn't even get to bust any heads," Chief called out to the rest of us as we hopped on our rides. I chuckled at that.

"Don't worry, I have a feeling this isn't over just yet."

"You know we have your back, Surfer dude!" Fuckin' Chief.

"I'm headed to go see Gillian. Let me know if there's anything on the audio worth listening to," I told Ghost. It wasn't really my place to listen in to that as the officers of the club would handle it. Considering it might concern my woman and her kid, he understood my interest though.

"You know we will," he informed me and then he was off in the opposite direction from where I was going. My woman was back in her home now that it had been fixed and a security system had been put in. I was actually looking forward to just being able to crash and relax with her for a while tonight before I had to slip out so that Kade wouldn't find me there in the morning. Not that it really mattered since they had spent a few nights at the clubhouse. Kade was now firmly in my corner as the only man his momma should be dating.

That wasn't true. He had gotten to ride on the backs of a few of the guys bikes with them during the time he was staying with us and I'm pretty sure he didn't care which one of us dated his mom so long as he was able to get rides now and again. I chuckled at the thought as I pulled in to see my woman and let her know it was all over – for now.

18. TOO SOON

THE PHONE IN MY POCKET RANG JUST AS WE WERE CALLED UP TO head out to a pickup. "No rush, guys. You're scooping a DOA," our boss informed us as we hopped into the bus. My usual partner was out sick today, so Dave was filling in for her. "I'll drive," he insisted. It had been two months since our meet with Tonka and to his credit, nothing had gone down. Joe seemed to be on the short leash Tonka promised us he was on, and all had gone back to normal again.

Fine by me since my cell was ringing again. I picked it up and saw that I'd already missed two calls from Gillian. "Hey baby, what's up?"

"Oh God, Gray!" Her voice was weak and broken.

"Gillian? What's going on?"

"Gray, they knocked me out. I... I can't... shit, I can't get my legs to work."

"Change of plans, Dave. Call it in and let them know to send someone else for the DOA. We need to get to my woman, she's hurt."

"She needs to call it in to 911, man. You know policy."

"Baby, I need you tell me where you are."

"Home. I can't get my legs to work. I don't see Kade anywhere. Oh God, Gray, I think someone took Kade."

"Okay, baby, listen I'm calling it in. Got no choice. We're on our way to you now. Just sit tight."

"Gray, don't hang up, please!" She begged me.

"I'm not going anywhere baby, I promise."

I rattled off Gillian's address to Dave. "Go! She says she was hit on the head and can't move her legs."

"Fuck!" Dave called out as he threw the lights and sirens on and turned us around.

I got on the radio and called it in and then I grabbed Dave's phone and called Smoke while I was on the line on my cell with Gillian. "Yo!" He answered.

"Smoke, someone attacked Gillian. I'm in the bus on my way to her house now. Need to get someone out there now. She can't see Kade."

"Did she look in the house?"

"She can't move her legs," I informed him. The panic over making that statement was started to set in. It could be just a temporary sign of a concussion but could also be more permanent and we wouldn't know until we could get her evaluated.

"Shit, on my way! I'll call Ghost."

I hung up and handed Dave his phone back. "Try not to worry, you know it's most likely temporary," he informed me of what I already knew.

"I know, and it's not helping." I put the phone back up to my ear. "Baby, you still with me?" No answer. "Gillian?" I called out her name, louder this time. Still no answer. I turned the phone and glanced down seeing that the call had been dropped. "Damn it!" I called her back but didn't get an answer. "We need to hurry up, dude. She ain't picking her phone up."

"Almost there."

When we pulled up Smoke was already there hopping off his bike and running to Gillian who was lying on the ground. It appeared that she was unconscious. "Not a good fuckin' sign," I hissed out as I jumped from the bus before Dave had it parked.

"Jesus!" I heard him yell, but I was at a dead run heading toward Gillian. Dave took his time, gathering the equipment I should have been grabbing.

"Gray," she whispered.

"Oh, thank fuck!" I slid in beside her, remembering only at the last minute not to touch or move her head or neck. "I need you to stay still, baby. Don't try to turn your head."

"That's good, because I get sick every time I attempt to look around."

"I know. We're going to put a collar around your neck, slide a backboard under you, and then lift you onto the bus, okay baby?"

"What about Kade?"

"Don't worry about Kade, we'll find him," Smoke told her.

"What if they're hurting him?"

"Gillian, I need you to listen to me. The guys are on it. They're going to get him back, but right now we need to take care of you so you can give him a big hug to welcome him back home. Okay?"

"I'm scared, Gray."

"I know, baby. Just hang in there while we get you to the hospital okay?"

I worked on taking her vitals and doing what needed to be done as Dave drove us. Smoke hadn't come along and was coordinating search efforts to look for Kade. Never in my life had I felt so torn or completely helpless. It didn't take long for us to get to the hospital emergency room and get Gillian unloaded. Since she worked with the hospital closely for her job there had already been people waiting there to help with her.

"Hey, Gillie-Bean," one of the nurses called. "How are you feeling?"

"Like the lights are going to fry my retinas," she announced weakly.

"Aw, we'll get you in a dark space just as quick as we can, hon. Hang in there." She glanced around then. "Where's Kade? Is he okay?"

Gillian burst into tears then. "I... don't... know," she got out in a blubbering mess. The nurse turned to me then.

"What's going on?"

"It's being handled. We think Kade's father snatched him."

"Oh my God! No!"

I waved her off. "There are people looking for him right now. When we were on our way to get her, Gillian was complaining about not being able to get her legs to work right. When we arrived on scene she told me she felt like she was going to be sick every time she tried to look around."

"Did you tell her not to look around?" The nurse asked this while knowing I worked on an ambulance.

"Of fucking course, I did. She had tried to move to look for Kade when she first regained consciousness, before we got there."

She had the good sense to look sheepish as she shrugged her shoulders. "Sorry, not all the guys in your position do their jobs right."

"This one is a dream to work with," another of the staff commented. "Good to see you, Gray."

"It'll be better if you can get my woman fixed up so we can get her out of here."

"Your woman?" The attending physician asked.

"Wow, Gillian, you've been keeping secrets. And a hot one at that!" The nurse chuckled, trying to engage Gillian who just moaned as a bright pen light was flashed in first one eye and then another.

"I can tell you now that due to the sickness and the inability to control the limbs we'll have to keep you overnight for observation," the physician – Kristen James – finally blurted out. We're going to get you back for a scan in just a minute to make sure there aren't any underlying issues that may cause a bigger problem. You both know how this works."

"Sure," I answered.

"Gray, call Beth, please."

"I'll do that, baby."

"No, listen, call Beth and get her to come out here so you know I'm not alone. Then I need you to go find my son."

I leaned in and placed a gentle kiss on her forehead. "Are you sure you don't want me here with you?"

"No, I want you to bring Kade back to me. That's the most important thing. Beth can update you while you look."

"I'll find him. I promise you, between me and the club, we won't stop until he's found and the assholes responsible for this pay!"

"I did not hear that last part," Doc Kristen announced. "For the record though, an extra punch to the junk wouldn't be too much to ask, would it?"

"That goes for me too," the nurse called out as she came back to the bedside with an extra blanket in tow. It was good that she noticed Gillian was shivering. I wasn't sure if it was because she was actually cold, as it was chilly in here, or if it was because she was going into shock. I glanced up at Doc.

"We've got her, go do your thing."

I turned to find Dave standing there. "Shit, I forgot..." I huffed the words out. I was in the middle of a goddamn 24-hour shift.

"Don't worry, I called in Barry. He's coming to take your spot. Cleared it with management since this was an emergency."

"You're a damn life saver. Beers on me when this is all over."

"Gray!" Gillian called me just before I ran out the door.

"Yeah, baby?"

"I could have sworn I heard a woman's voice too before I was hit."

That was a bit of a shocker. "Okay, I'll let the guys know. Love you, Gillian!"

"I must have a traumatic brain injury, because I could have sworn you just told me you love me," she muttered.

"I did tell you, and I plan on telling you a whole lot more, so you get better while I go get Kade."

"I love you too," she finally muttered, but then her eyes shut.

"Don't worry, we gave her a little something for the pain. It will knock her out for a bit. We'll rouse her in just a while."

I didn't stick around after that. I had a job to do and I damn sure couldn't rest until it was done, because there was no way I was leaving Kade in the hands of the psycho or psychos who would do this shit. I shot a text out to Smoke before I left.

> Surfer: Gillian says she thought she heard a woman's voice before she got knocked out. Not sure what that means, but we need to check with the grandmother and Joe's ex-wife.

> Smoke: On it, brother.

> Surfer: Beth is staying with Gillian. I'm headed to the clubhouse. Checking in with Ghost and then I'm helping find my kid.

> Smoke: Check with Ghost, then we'll meet up.

19. HIDE AND SEEK

I NO SOONER LAUNCHED MYSELF OFF MY BIKE HEADING FOR THE clubhouse than Ghost was plowing through the doors. "Get your ass back on, we're headed to see Tonka," he ordered.

I didn't hesitate to comply. "You think he's going to bother to get involved?"

"He'll get involved, because I'm about to force the issue."

We rode the fifteen miles toward the southern edge of the town where Tonka and his boys had a shitty little compound style setup. We were escorted inside the gates and then taken directly to a sparsely furnished room that was most likely used as an office when it was needed. Judging by the thick layer of dust around the place, it wasn't needed often.

"Ghost, Surfer," Tonka greeted each of us. "To what do I owe this fine honor today?"

"We have a kid missing and a woman in the hospital," Ghost informed him.

Tonks appeared puzzled for just a moment before aware-ness slid down his features. "Fuck. You know for sure it was Joe?"

Ghost nodded, confirming what I only speculated about up until now. "Have security footage at the house. He was there with a woman wearing a long blond wig. Can't identify her because her face was obscured by the hair and glasses. It was definitely your man though, down to the tattoo on his forearm." Ghost tossed a picture onto the desk in front of Tonka, sending up a plume of dust in the man's face.

"Shit," he yelled out waiving the offending particles away from his face. "This fuckin pig sty," he muttered before glancing down at the picture. Then he pulled out his cell phone and did some quick typing. "Give me just a minute, boys. I'll have some information for you. About all I can give is places you might want to check where he could be hiding out. Thing is, we're gonna check too. We find the kid; we'll call and hand him over. We find them first, and Joe is going to suffer by our hands."

"You find him first, you make sure no harm comes to my kid!" I seethed at him. "Then you wait, because if I don't get my justice, I'll be coming for every single one of you mother fuckers."

"Surfer!" Ghost called out to get me in line. Then he turned to Tonka. "He's obviously pretty fuckin' upset. His woman's lying in the hospital right now and kid's God knows where."

"I get it. We'll make sure old Joe's still breathing." Before anything else could be said a man limped into the room. "You got what I asked for, Squirrel?"

"Yeah, um, yes. Yes sir, right here," the kid stammered. He couldn't have been more than twenty, and I didn't think he was that old. Scrawny with a think patchwork beard sprouting on his face, the kid glanced over and I could literally smell the fear rolling off of him. "Well, hand it over, boy," Tonka yelled.

"S-s-sorry." He then slid some papers into Tonka's hand and stepped back quickly. I'd dare say it had been a tactical retreat, and I wasn't the only one to notice. Ghost slid his eyes from the boy to me and then tipped his chin ever so slightly. Yep, we'd be finding out if the boy was being held here against his will or abused in any way. Honestly, it wasn't on the top of my radar though. My personal priority was finding Kade and bringing him home safe and sound. The longer he was gone out there, the less likely I'd be able to bring him home unharmed. His father was clearly off his rocker, and who knew what would set him off. Maybe a kid screaming for his mother?

Once the kid left the room Ghost spoke up. "Kid's jumpy to be a prospect."

Tonka laughed. "Squirrel ain't no fuckin' prospect. I got landed with my brother's kid when he bit it." Tonka shook his head looking disappointed. "Squirrel was on the bike at the time. Brain bucket saved him, but it didn't save him, if you catch my drift." He knocked a finger into the side of his own head. He's a bit touched now, squirrely, and has that limp. Don't know what else to do with him 'cept give him some bitch work to do like fetching shit." He tipped his head to the papers he handed to Ghost. "That should be every bit we have on Joe. The ex's address, his mom's place, a hunting cabin about 30 miles outside of town, and not much else. Bastard doesn't even have his own place to stay. He's always surfing a couch here or with one of the brothers since his old lady kicked him out a couple years ago.

"Before we head out, you wanna tell me how that leash broke?" Ghost asked Tonka.

Tonka's face took on a reddened hue. "Fuckin prospect we had tailing him ain't worth a shit," he grumbled. Joe ain't even the ripest banana in the bunch, but he managed to give the idiot the slip." He turned to his eyes from me back to Ghost. "Would have put another man on him, but my club has its own shit goin' down. I couldn't spare nobody else."

Ghost tipped his chin at the man and then moved to the door. I followed behind, waiting until we clear of the Hell's Hounds compound before I started sending out addresses to people. "Get Wren and Tuck to head to the cabin. I think we'll find that those two can get there the quickest. We'll head to the grandmother's place," Ghost informed me. "Smoke and Chief can hit the ex-wife's place. Send the messages, and let's go. We've already burned enough daylight here."

Two hours later, all the places on Tonka's list had been searched and there wasn't any sign of a kid being brought there, or Joe having been at any of them recently. My gut was spinning with anxiety though as Ghost and I got ready to leave the grandmother's place. We were gone, off to meet up with the others back at the clubhouse when I happened to think of something. I pulled over into a supermarket parking lot and turned to Ghost.

"When we were leaving a glare of light blasted me in the eye just as I was backing the bike up."

"Yeah, the windows from the basement in the house next door reflected light up at me too."

"There wasn't a basement in the grandmother's house was there?"

"Didn't see an access anywhere," Ghost muttered, but his wheels were turning in the same direction mine were.

"We have to get back there, now!"

Nothing more was said, we hauled ass back down the road and pulled into the drive. The older woman came out looking none too happy with us being back. "What are you doing back here? Do I need to call the police? I won't tolerate this type of harassment."

"You should definitely call the police," I informed her before turning to Ghost. "What's the standard stint for aiding and abetting a kidnapping?"

"Pretty sure that's a hefty haul in the big house," Ghost confirmed.

"I'm thinking I heard it's a three-year minimum and up to 10 years here in this fine state."

"Nobody's been kidnapped here," she hissed out.

"Yeah, okay, so then you wouldn't mind us taking another look around the house?"

"I do mind," she argued.

"Too fuckin' bad, lady. You failed to tell us about that basement you have."

"I don't have a basement," she argued.

Ghost pulled out a Glock and aimed it at her. "Get in the

fuckin' house and show us where the goddamn basement is. I just ran all the way out of patience with you."

"You can't do this," she sputtered. Ghost approached her, snagged her arm up and twisted it behind her back in a carry hold, and then escorted her bodily back into her house. "I think you'll find I can do whatever the fuck I want when you're hiding Gray's boy from us."

"I ain't hiding no one here, least of all any kid of his."

"What about your own grandson?"

She flinched at that but said nothing. "Where is the entrance to the basement?" She thought about holding out the information, but as soon as Ghost put the barrel of his gun to her temple she stuck her aged hand out and pointed toward a closet in the living room. I knew it was a closet because we had looked in there before. It was filled with a bunch of shit. Though, I was noticing some of that shit had been moved out into the living room since we left.

I went over and started tossing things from the little room until finally a trap door style basement access was revealed in the floor. "Holy fuck," I murmured as I pulled the door and dove damn near head first into the room below. What I saw when I got down there floored me. Kade was there with a fucking dirty rag stuffed in his mouth, but that was actually to be expected in a way. What had my head spinning was who was down there with him.

"Kayla?"

"Oh, thank God you found us!" She shrieked. "I've been down here with this kid for so long..."

What. The. Fuck?

Kade was shaking his head back and forth so hard I

thought he might hurt himself. I could also see the tension in Kayla's face and shoulders. Come here, Kade!" I called out.

"What about me? Aren't you going to come rescue me?"

I pointed the Barretta I'd had with me right at her. "Come on, son, get over here and let me get that shit off of you."

"Son? How dare you call that little shit your son. He's nothing."

"Oh yeah? Thought he was a prisoner here just like you?"

She narrowed her eyes on me. "So? That still doesn't mean I'm going to tolerate you laying claim to that little shit."

As soon as the rag was pulled free from his mouth Kade started talking frantically. "She hit my mom. She hurt my mom, Gray. Did you find her yet?"

"We got her, buddy. She's in the hospital getting checked out, but she'll be okay." Kade pointed his finger at Kayla. "She's the bad woman. She took me here. There's a man too. He was talking to my grandma, and she knew who he was." Kade's voice grew quieter. "I think he's the man that is supposed to be my dad. I don't want him to be, Gray. He's just as mean as that lady over there."

"All good down there?" Ghost called out from up above us.

"I have Kade. He's okay. I also have Kayla down here?"

"Kayla? What the fuck? Your Kayla?" Her face was smug as Ghost called her that.

"Not mine," I growled. "It is the bitch I scraped off though."

I heard Ghost chuckle at that, just in time to see Kayla launch herself. She wasn't aiming for me though. She was aiming for the kid. "They can't have you!" She screamed. "You were supposed to be mine!" I quickly pushed Kade behind me and took the brunt of her attack. She had something sharp in her hand and it sliced through the leather of my cut near my shoulder, beyond the shirt I wore underneath and straight through my skin with a flash of white-hot pain. My natural instinct was to shoot her, but the whimper behind me stilled my finger and instead I slammed the butt of my gun right into her temple. With any luck that killed her and I could tell Kade that she would wake up in the hospital just like his mom.

Ghost came down the stairs after having tied up Kade's grandmother. "Jesus, are you okay?" he asked.

"She was going to stab him," I told Ghost before turning to pick Kade up into my arms.

"Did you kill the bad lady?"

"No, bud. She's just sleeping right now. She'll wake up later." Kade started to shake in my arms.

"She's gonna get me again?"

"Fuck!" I heard Ghost hiss. "No!" I told him vehemently. "She will never come near you again. You know what's going to happen when she wakes up?" He shook his head back and forth as he clung to me. "She's going to go to jail for a really long time." It was the best lie I had to feed him. The bitch wouldn't be going to jail, though I wasn't entirely sure what we were going to be doing with her. Ghost was zip tying her hands together as I moved to get Kade out of the basement.

"It wasn't until I grabbed onto the ladder like steps that I remembered I'd just had my shoulder sliced into. The pain burned as I gritted my teeth and sucked it up. Once at the top

I had sweat beaded all over my forehead from the effort it took to carry a kid up those steps with the wound I had.

"Ghost!" I called out to him as I gently put Kade down when I felt the hot flush that generally signaled someone was about to pass out. I kneeled down and put my head between my legs to try to stave off the feeling and prevent myself from going down.

"What's up?" Ghost asked as he made his way up the stairs.

"Gray is bleeding," Kade pointed out.

"Sorry, felt faint and didn't want him up here alone just in case someone else made an appearance."

"No worries, I put in a call to Wren and Smoke. Smoke and Chief are almost here." Ghost went digging around in the woman's house until he managed to come back with some peroxide and bandages. "I know I don't have your skills, or even Smoke's, but let's see if we can't get this patched up just a little bit." I removed my kutte, and had Kade hold it for me. Then Ghost helped cut my shirt off of me because it was too much to pull my arm up to get the thing off.

"It's cut," Kade mentioned. I thought he was talking about my arm, but when I glanced over at him I noticed him fingering the slice through the leather.

"Your old man's gonna fix it later, and now his kutte will have a battle scar." He winked at Kade. "It'll make him look more like a bad-ass biker and less like a surfer dude, finally."

Kade grinned then. "You get to look bad-ass, Gray."

"Hey kid," I chided.

"Don't tell my mom," he whispered causing both Ghost

and I to chuckle. Unfortunately, the movement hurt and I winced in pain. "I won't tell her you cried either," he informed me.

"Emotional blackmail. Isn't that step one on the road to becoming a biker?" I asked Ghost who chuckled once again.

"The kid is well on his way," he agreed about the same time Smoke and Chief showed up.

After I was temporarily patched up, we packed Kade up and took him back to the clubhouse with me. Once we were there he refused to leave me side, even as Smoke took me to a back room and got ready to fix me up the right way, and for the second time since I had joined his motorcycle club, the man sewed me up. "This is becoming a nasty habit with you, Surfer. Before long I'll be stitching better than a plastic surgeon," he teased.

"If only," I countered on a wince as he brought a needle back through my skin once more.

"Can we go see my mom when you're done?"

"Sure, we can, little dude. Let Smoke make my stitches look extra pretty first, okay? Don't want your mom thinking I'm ugly now."

Kade laughed. "She thinks you're pretty hot," he admitted.

"Oh yeah? How do you know?"

"I heard her and Ms. Beth talking about you and Hold 'Em. They said you were both hotter than the fires Mr. Smoke puts out."

That had Smoke throwing his head back and laughing so deeply I thought he might bust a gut and need some stitching up, himself. "Hotter than the fires I put out," he muttered while still cackling.

"Dude," I called out to Kade. He just shrugged at me.

"What? That's what they said."

"Come on, little dude, let's go remind your mom how hot I am."

"She's going to be surprised to see me."

"She sure is, buddy."

20. THE REUNION

Kade and I made our way to the room Gillian had been admitted to. I went without my kutte since I still had to clean it up and patch the fucker back together. Though, I was grateful of the thing since it probably saved me from a much deeper slice, and possibly nerve damage and mobility issues. I shivered to think about what would have happened if I hadn't managed to get Kade shoved behind me quick enough. That crazy cunt had seriously intended to stab the kid.

"Knock, knock," I called out as I pushed the door open to Gillian's room.

"Gray!" She called out and then her eyes found Kade's. "Kade! Oh God baby, I'm so happy to see you!" She held out her arms and he went running for his mom.

"Told you she'd be happy to see me."

"Of course, I'm happy to see you, baby. I was so worried."

"That mean woman tried to stab me, but Gray stopped her. She stabbed him instead."

Gillian's worried eyes widened in shock as she scanned them all over me. "What?"

"It's okay, G. We're both all good. He's perfectly fine, and I'll be okay. Just a scratch."

"Nuh-uh. It bled a lot, and Mr. Smoke had to sew him up like you did with my shirt that time I ripped the big hole in it," the kid blabbered to his mom. I winced. Busted.

"You're going to tell me all about it later," she informed me. I just nodded my head in acknowledgment. "Right now, I just want great big hugs from my boys." Kade leaned in and squeezed his mom hard. I saw her pale and stepped in immediately.

"Okay, little dude, I think mom's quite ready for those powerful hugs of yours. How about being gentle. She got her head hurt today, and it makes her feel yucky when she moves around too much, okay?"

He gently slid from his mom's lap and backed up to lean against my legs. "Sorry, mom."

"It's okay, baby. Worth it for one of your hugs."

"No, I don't want to hurt you. Not ever. You're the best mom ever." Kade glanced up at me then. "Gray came to remind you how hot he is." He leaned over a little and cupped his hand around his mouth before whispering the rest loud enough that still heard. "Mr. Smoke gave him ugly stitches even though Gray lied and said he did a beautiful job. He said you might think he was ugly now. You shouldn't think that, mom, because Gray's the best dad, and I want to keep him."

I swear, my heart stopped beating for a minute there, before it kicked in double time. I glanced over at Gillian for her response, because surely I'd just heard him wrong. She offered me a watery smile as tears spilled over onto her cheeks. "Don't worry, honey, we're definitely keeping Gray."

"Are you going to marry him?"

"Do you think he wants to marry me?" she asked, but she wasn't looking at her son. Her eyes were locked with mine.

"More than you know," I responded.

"Well, I guess it's official then," she announced.

"Yeah! My mom and dad are getting married!" Kade shouted into the room which in turn woke Beth who had fallen asleep in the chair on the other side of the bed. Gillian giggled, and it was the most beautiful sound I'd ever heard.

"You're getting married?" Beth asked.

Wait. Was that for real? "Um," I started to say but Gillian just grinned at me from her where she had lain her head back down on her pillow. "Yeah, it's the only way to prove Gray's still hot even with the stitches."

"What?" Beth asked incredulously.

"Yeah, can't go around hurting a guy's ego after he's been wounded in battle," I added.

"Wounded? Battle? What battle? How did I miss the two of you getting engaged?" Beth reached over Gillian and grabbed hold of her hand. "Where's the ring?"

"We have to go pick it out as soon as she's sprung from this joint," I informed her. Why not? Life was short. No one knew that better than the four people sitting in this room. Besides, there was no way I was disappointing my son. He had just passed biker 101 after all. He was an emotional manipulation champion, and he proved this further when he winked at me. Yup, the little shit winked. He knew exactly what he'd been doing.

We stayed visiting for a while before Beth offered to take Kade back to the clubhouse so I could stick around with Gillian since visiting hours were over with. I had already informed the nurses that I wasn't going to be leaving until she could come home with me.

A knock on the door a couple hours later startled me awake and I felt the tug on the stitches as I came up from the chair with a jolt. "Fuck!" I hissed as I stood and moved to the door. Smoke stood there with Ghost.

"Mind if we come in?"

I glanced up and down the hall wondering how the hell they got past the nurse from hell who had shouted about visiting hours being over for an hour and a half earlier. Ghost grinned. "My old lady is a nurse. She knows most of these women too even though she only works part time these days."

I opened the door wider so they could both come in and we all three converged toward the back of the room away from Gillian. "What's going on?"

"We got a hold of Joe," Ghost told me. "Not much left of him, I'm afraid, since his own club got hold of him first."

"I was afraid of that," I admitted.

"They took his ink, beat him to within an inch of his life and then made the call. Honestly, not sure we can keep him from meeting his fuckin' maker much longer at this point."

"Wanted to give you the option of having one of us sit with her while you go deal that blow, or..."

I shook my head. "I'm not leaving her. Just knowing he's

gone will be plenty for me. What about Kayla though? Did you get anything out of her?"

"Yeah, that bitch is one bat-shit crazy psycho!" Smoke shook his head in disbelief. "The shit she was spouting, you would think the two of you were getting ready to walk down the aisle to your happily ever after or something."

I grinned. "Well, she definitely isn't the one I'll be meeting at the end of an aisle soon," I mentioned.

"What? For real?" Smoke asked.

I turned to Ghost. "That kid, he passed biker 101 in a big way. Called me the best dad ever and told his mom she couldn't see my stitches and think I was ugly now because Mr. Smoke didn't do a good job." Both men started to chuckle.

"Smooth little shit, there."

"Yeah, no kidding," I agreed with Ghost.

"Obviously, it was all said in fun," Smoke offered me the out.

"I don't want that out, brother. They're mine. As soon as we're both ready and able we're going to be walking down that aisle."

"Good for you," Ghost told me as he clapped a hand on my good shoulder. "Congrats, man. She's a good woman. Besides, we won't have to look too far for recruits in a few years." I chuckled at that. I was fairly certain we'd have our hands full keeping Kade out of shit with the MC until he was old enough.

"So, how did Kayla end up in all this mess with Joe?"

"She was sleeping with him. Dumb bitch went to be club pussy for the Hounds. She must have seen his tat and put two and two together about who he was. I guess she thought she'd get in good with their club if she helped Joe out. She followed your woman home from Beth's house, and took the opportunity for what it was. Called Joe and told him they were unprotected at her house. He showed up, got her outside, and Kayla hit her over the head with something. From the sounds of Kayla's whining, Joe really was just there to talk some sense into Gillian about allowing him to get to know Kade. Kayla escalated everything when she hit Gillian over the head though so Joe took the boy and hid him with his mom. Kayla came by later to scoop him up, but didn't make it out in time before you guys showed back up."

"Good thing we did, considering she was ready to stab him in front of me."

"Yeah, she did not have healthy things to say about the kid. I'll leave it at that because you don't need that shit playing out in your head," Smoke informed me. I couldn't disagree with him. I could already imagine plenty. There was no reason to add to it.

Ghost glanced down at his phone after we heard it vibrate. "Looks like we're too late if you did want a piece of Joe. He's gone."

"Damn," I muttered. "Not that I cared to get a piece of him since he had already been dealt with, but one day I'm gonna have to tell little dude that not only was his dad that piece of shit who kidnapped him, but that he's also dead as a result."

"No, you're gonna tell him that his dad is the man who cared for him and his momma. The piece of shit who donated some sperm is dead, and there's nothing to miss," Ghost amended for me.

"We do need to know something though before we go." Smoke glanced between Ghost and myself. "What do you want us to do with the crazy bitch?"

I ran my hand through my hair and blew out a frustrated breathe. "As much as I'd like to take the easy way out with that, we can't. Her dad is a powerful man, and while he's washed his hands of her he also keeps tabs on her, hoping that she'll get better. If she were to suddenly disappear, I can't imagine anything good would come of it and it would cast a shadow over the MC the likes of which might have feds breathing down our necks and up our assholes."

"Shit!" Ghost hissed out.

"Yeah, let me handle it. I'll give her father a call and fill him in on the fact that she just kidnapped and tried to kill a little kid, stabbed me, and whatever the fuck else she has going on right now. I have a feeling he'll see to it that she's locked away where she won't be able to hurt anyone again."

"You think we can trust that he'll do that?"

"I know we can. He's had a facility picked out for her since she fucked over one of his friends and colleagues. He gave her a second chance at her mom's behest, but he's been waiting for her to fall apart again."

"All right, you handle that, but when he comes to pick her up, I want to deal with the man and get some personal assurances too. Don't want that bitch coming back to bite us in the ass."

"That works for me, man."

EPILOGUE

A WEEK LATER, KAYLA'S FATHER CAME TO PICK HIS DAUGHTER UP from Cedar Falls and take her back to California where she'd then be boarding a flight to somewhere in another country where they weren't afraid to treat their patients with cutting edge torture techniques. It wasn't a pretty place, and it was clear that Kayla's father wasn't doing this because he cared about his daughter. He was doing this as a form of retribution for all the problems she'd caused him. She would probably wish sooner than later that we had just ended her instead.

We maintained the insurance policy on her though. If we caught wind that she'd arrived in country again we wouldn't hesitate to put her down one way or another. We had enough on her including video of her at the clubhouse sucking a brother's cock who wasn't her man, and video footage of her bashing Gillian's head and running off with another biker who stole a kid. Kayla's father knew we had all of it because he'd seen it with his own two eyes. He assured us he did not want any of it going public, and that Kayla would never be heard from again.

Gillian and I discussed getting married quickly, but neither of us liked the idea. We were taking our time and planning things out. She wore my ring though. It was the one she'd picked the day after she came home from the hospital. The club was having a barbecue to celebrate our family being free of the turmoil we'd been through over the past few months from all of our drama, the loss of Bender and Sophie, and then the shit with Poppy's ex-husband showing up and trying to win her back. For once, we were all breathing easy and free. We also had Leanne's cherished triple chocolate cake and Poppy's ribs to look forward to. Life was good.

"Hey, G?" I called out for my woman from where I was standing over by the beer coolers on the top tier of the deck.

"What, honey?" she called back from the lawn where she had been just been chasing Kade and Abby around.

"Come on up here a minute. Bring the little dude with you."

"Wittle Doood," Brantley mocked from beside me.

"Come here squirt," Smoke called out to his nephew.

"I wansta playz with wittle doood, Unc Moke."

Damn, but that kid was cute. Gillian and Kade came to stand beside me and I pulled out a big white box to hand to Gillian. "G, my woman, my old lady, don't you think it's time to make this shit official?"

"What? I thought we did that with this?" She held up her hand so that the diamond in the center winked as the sunlight hit it.

"Yeah, baby, but I'm a biker. We do shit different," I told her.

"Yeah, mom. Geez. Bikers do shi-stuff different." Kade was at least smart enough to curb that mouth when his mother was side-eyeing him. Still, the kid thought he was working through his prospecting period already.

"Hey, wittle dooood, wanna playz wif me?" Brantley asked as he tugged on Kade's shirt. Kade glanced down and smiled at the little boy.

"Sure, Brant, just give me a minute to see what kind of present my mom got."

"Open it so our son can go play," I told her. I watched as her eyes grew wet. It touched her every time I laid claim to Kade, but it had to pale in comparison to that first time he'd called me his dad.

We watched as Gillian tore into the box and then reverently ran her hands over the object inside. She glanced up at me and I watched as some of that wetness trailed down her cheeks. "Well?" Poppy called out excitedly. "What did you, get? Show us! Show us!" That woman! Smoke had his hands full. She managed to get everyone, including Kade and Brantley in on the action.

"Show us! Show us!" The chant went on until Gillian pulled the buttery soft leather out of the box and held it up for everyone to see. The back of her kutte had the same logo the brothers wore, including the top rocker for Aces High MC. The bottom rocker simply said Old Lady. She turned it to show everyone and I heard the gasp she made as she read the name patch I'd had embroidered just for her. "G -Property of Surfer"

"Whoa!" Kade spoke excitedly as he reached out to touch the kutte. "Mom, this means you're part of the club now!"

"Yeah it does, buddy," she answered him as I helped her put it on. "I love it, Gray."

"I love you," I told her just before my lips met hers.

"Eww, gross," Kade announced.

"Ooo, theyz kissin'." Brantley announced. "Theyz kissin' like you kisseded Popwee."

"Yeah, Brant. You'll be there some day."

"Nope. Girls awe toopid." As if to prove his point Beth leaned in too far with Abby and she managed to grab hold of a chunk of Brantley's hair. "Owie!" He yelped as Abby giggled. The boy turned a furiously mean mug her way. "See, toopid girl."

As weird as it may sound, all of that just made me long for the time when I could put a baby in Gillian's belly. She deserved to have a pregnancy with a man by her side and I couldn't wait to watch her grow heavy with our child and then to have Kade as the best big brother ever. Shit. I needed to marry her sooner than we were planning.

"Kade Thomas!" Ghost called out.

Kade startled and then walked the few steps to where Ghost was standing. "Don't think anyone forgot about you today, son."

"Um," Kade started to say as he turned desperate eyes to me wondering what was going on and why he was in trouble.

"You are a cool kid," Ghost started which perked Kade right up. He turned his full attention back to Ghost again. "When you were taken, you stayed especially cool under pressure, and you had your dad's back when he needed you to with those ugly stitches. Your mom would have left him, for sure, if you hadn't convinced her not to."

Kade was beaming, and I was doing my best to hold my laughter in. Fuckin' Ghost. "So, it's with great honor that I bestow you with this," he pulled a hand out from behind his back and held out a kutte that was the perfect size for Kade. The back logo, again, was the same with the Aces High MC rocker. The bottom rocker simply stated, 'future member'.

"You grow out of that one, and we'll talk promotion, kid!"

"Mom, Dad, do you see this?" He bounced up and down excitedly. "I'm a member now, too!"

Meeting Kayla had been the best thing that ever happened to me, because she brought me to my family. I'd always be thankful for that. Some people's purpose in our lives never really becomes clear, but for that moment. I sent up a thank you for whatever fates made it possible that I was standing here today with a whole family full of brothers, my woman, and my kid soaking up the good vibes and putting all the nightmares behind us.

THANKS FOR READING PROVEN, book #3 in the Aces High MC - Cedar Falls Series

Please read/review the book, as this is how other readers find the books you love.

Don't forget to check out the other books in the Aces High MC - Cedar Falls Series.

- Redemption Weather
- Smoke and the Flame

Don't forget to sign up for my newsletter, so you never miss a new release!

https://christineandanne.myflodesk.com/newsletter

ALSO BY CHRISTINE MICHELLE

CHRISTINE MICHELLE

Kings of Anarchy MC: New Mexico

Property of Bigfoot

Aces High MC – Dakotas

Dancing with Danger · Whiskey Tango Foxtrot · The Restart and the Remedy

Aces High MC – Charleston

The Other Princess · A Love So Hard · The Princess and the Prospect · The Killing Ride · A Twist of Fate · Everlasting · A Year and a Day ·The Broken Beginning – Part One ·The Broken Beginning – Part Two

Aces High MC – Tallahassee

Crushed

Aces High MC – Sierra High

Walker · Trouble

Aces High MC – Cedar Falls

Redemption Weather · Proven · Smoke and the Flame · Redemption Duet Box Set

S.H.E. MC

Angel Girl · JoJo · Keys

Robeson Family Novels (standalones)

The Forgotten Wife · When the Last Petal Falls · A Different Husband

Standalone Novels

The Groupie Journal

Letters to Lily

His Bittersweet Regret

Bad at Love

TFO

The Fortunate Ones

T.I.E. Series

The Infinite Something · The Infinite Beat

Valhalla Rising

Revived

Dark Leopards MC (paranormal)

Ridden by Darkness · The B Team

Mirage Island Mates

Into the Grasslands · Beyond the Grasslands

Seasons Pack Series

Winter Wolves

The Ancients Series

Shadows of the Ancients · Falling into the White · Branches of the Willow
· Bound by the Moon

Vukodlak Brew Series

Entwined · Enraged

The Awakening Series

Birthrights · Revelations · Incarnations

Death Viewers

Breathless

Upper YA Titles

The Voodoo Follies (PNR)

Catch a Falling Star (Dystopian Romance)

ANNE STORM

Savage Vipers MC

Wait For Me · Devastate Me · Surprise Me · Baby Me

Loved for the Holidays

Cupid Broke My Heart · Ghosted by Texas · Resolving Rumors

Cheating Hearts Series

The Homewrecker's Fate · The Regrettable Mistake

ABOUT THE AUTHOR - CM

Christine Michelle runs on coffee and giggles as she writes her angst-fueled romance stories (motorcycle club, rockstar, paranormal, college, & other contemporary as well as women's fiction and marriage in trouble novels).
She is a mom to four humans (2 girls, 2 boys – all grown now).
When she's not writing books, she enjoys reading, drawing, hiking, or feeding her soul with live music at concerts.
Christine is a traveler and has lived all over the USA (and

other parts of the world). She currently lives in San Antonio, TX with her two fur babies.

Universal links to everything
(website, social media, book links, and more)
https://linktr.ee/christinemichelle

facebook.com/M00nlitDreams

instagram.com/christinemichelle_annestorm

tiktok.com/@christine.michelle.books

www.ingramcontent.com/pod-product-compliance
Lightning Source LLC
Chambersburg PA
CBHW020634260626
47157CB00008B/2737